Please return/renew this item
by the last date shown.
Books can also be renewed at
www.bolton.gov.uk/libraries

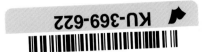

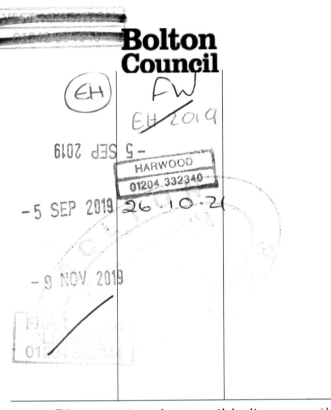

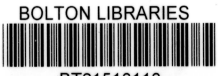

The Flames of Alvorado

Matt Brogan, wrongly imprisoned for the murder of his wife and son, escapes to go in search of the real killers whose evidence brought about his conviction.

In the remote town of Alvorado, a hideaway for outlaws on the run and the power base of the McLagan family, Brogan links up with lawman Jed Harding and the pair set out to rid the territory of the rule of fear.

When hot-headed Roy McLagan sets out to burn the farmers from their homes, Brogan and Harding persuade the locals to fight back. But to bring an end to the killings Brogan has to call on help from an unlikely source – Alex McLagan, the man he had vowed to kill.

By the same author

Guns of Virtue
Gannon's Law
A Bullet for Ben McCabe
Shadow of the Noose
No Peace for a Rebel
Dig Two Graves
The Last Gun

The Flames of Alvorado

Peter Wilson

A Black Horse Western

ROBERT HALE

First published in Great Britain 2019

ISBN 978-0-7198-2969-7

The Crowood Press
The Stable Block
Crowood Lane
Ramsbury
Marlborough
Wiltshire SN8 2HR

www.bhwesterns.com

Robert Hale is an imprint
of The Crowood Press

Typeset by
Derek Doyle & Associates, Shaw Heath
Printed and bound in Great Britain by
4Bind Ltd, Stevenage, SG1 2XT

CHAPTER ONE

The blistering heat from the midday sun was becoming unbearable and Matt Brogan ran his arm across his forehead in an effort to stem the sweat. The prison clothes stuck to his aching limbs and the stench from the long line of unwashed bodies made him want to vomit.

But he had to hold his nerve. For weeks he had waited for this moment and the chance to escape the living hell that he had endured for almost three years.

Further along the line the crack of a whip and the coarse barking of orders beyond the capacity of flesh and blood to follow only served to strengthen his resolve.

Soon the guards would order a break for water. This was not an act of kindness from the brutes who patrolled the working parties but by order of the prison governor.

He did not want men to die too soon because of the heat and for want of a mug of water. For them death would mean escape from the punishment that had been handed out for their crimes that included rape, murder, bestiality and sodomy – all the sins that the Good Lord had decreed to be against His will in the Scriptures.

Governor Jacob Harper had his own creed, his own brand of justice. He was a Scriptures and Good Lord zealot and these men had been sent to him. They must survive to learn the errors of their ways and repent.

Matthew Brogan was one such man. He had been sentenced to fifteen years hard labour in the penitentiary for the brutal murder of his wife and son and the governor felt such evil worthy of his personal attention. Killing a woman was diabolical in itself but the murder of an innocent child was beyond human forgiveness. In Harper's eyes Brogan should have been hanged and his worthless body left on display as a warning to others but the judge had clearly allowed him to live for a purpose. And that purpose was for Harper to extend the killer's suffering.

One day he would allow Brogan to die. But that would not be today.

A single rifle shot signaled the start of a ten-minute drinks break and most of the men sank wearily to their knees, too exhausted to make the short walk to the nearest water wagon.

But Matt Brogan was not among them; he had other plans. Now was the time that the guards were also tired and thirsty, and growing ever more resentful at their work detail. Their attention was at its lowest. They were all weary of the same routine.

The biggest among them – the one they called Moose – was standing over Matt, his face full of hate for the prisoner he saw as lawman turned child killer.

'On your feet, dirt bag,' he snarled and leaned forward to spit in Brogan's face. Moose was a big man but he was stupid and he was careless. A broad grin revealing a row of broken and stained teeth spread across his face as he watched his prisoner cringe as if stricken by fear.

Brogan allowed himself to be dragged towards the water wagon and the sight of him being forced along the road was the signal for the rest of the working gang to strike. The planned fight broke out among the nearest group –

the first yell prompting Moose to lose his concentration on the man he had been taunting.

As the giant guard turned his attention to the developing brawl among the other prisoners, Matt took his chance. Mustering what strength he still had left, he took a firm grip on the rock he had dragged from the pile and smashed it onto Moose's head. Even a man the size of the guard was sent sprawling into the dirt, his whip falling from his grasp. Matt saw his chance, leaping over the pile of rocks at the side of the road and diving into the undergrowth eight feet down.

A rifle bullet flew over his head and shattered a branch on the nearest tree. Scrambling down the steep bank, Matt zig-zagged his way deep into the covering greenery. Up above, the guards rushed towards the fighting group, firing shots into the air but leaving others unwatched. Another rushed to help the stricken Moose but everywhere there was mayhem. Then. . . .

A young prison guard, on his first day of duty on the work patrol, fired blindly into the nearest group. A prisoner fell, clutching his stomach, others hurled a volley of stones in the direction of the guards. Another shot was fired. Then another. Suddenly there was silence. The prisoners stared down at the dying figure whose blood was seeping into the dust.

The riot was over.

One prisoner was lying dead. Another – Matthew Brogan – was on his way to freedom.

Slowly, silently, the guards rounded up the disparate group and began marching them back towards the penitentiary, where they would be deprived of food and water and confined to their cells while the God-fearing governor would blame them all and Matt Brogan for the death of the young man whose only crime had been to mix with the wrong people and who was due for release in a few weeks.

Far off, high on a distant ridge, a lone rider lowered his spyglass and leaned forward in the saddle. He allowed himself a smile of satisfaction as he watched the fugitive disappear into the undergrowth. Slowly he removed the badge from his shirt and slipped it into his pocket. The first stage of the plan was a success. The rider tugged on the horse's reins and set off down the slope.

Life in the penitentiary would go on as usual and every town in the hundreds of miles between the prison and the Mexican border would receive a poster bearing a picture of escaped prisoner Matthew Brogan, and the legend: Wanted For Murder. Reward $3,000 Dead or Alive.

Every town including Alvorado, where Law and Order were strangers.

Governor Jacob Harper would not lose a minute's sleep over the loss of Prisoner 8832. If the heat of the desert did not get him and leave him to the buzzards, then a bullet from the hundred and one bounty hunters would put him in an early grave. Yes, $3,000 was a small price to pay to rid the world of a man like Matthew Brogan.

The governor read again through the file he had on the man he had watched and hated for almost three years. A man who had killed his woman and child. He closed the file and slid it into a cabinet, which he slammed shut and settled down to the more important business of lunch.

CHAPTER TWO

The baking heat of the day had given way to a bitterly cold night under cloudless skies and Matt Brogan was in desperate need of clean and warm clothing to replace his prison rags. He also needed food to quell the hunger pains that had gripped him over the last few miles. He had no idea how far he had travelled since the breakout – or even if he was still in Colorado – but he had yet to come across any signs of life. His limbs still ached and the scratches that he had suffered while scrambling his way through the brambles were still weeping blood.

He had no plan other than to put as much distance between himself and the prison and then head for the town of Alvorado.

Matt had not made friends during his three years behind prison bars – a penitentiary was not the place to build friendships – but he had gathered enough information to know that he was risking his life heading into New Mexico and that if he was recognized that life would not be worth a nickel.

But what was his future anyway? Twelve more years in that hell, and after that an old age of lonely bitterness?

Finding a sheltered hideaway among the bushes, Matt

settled down and tried to sleep. But, despite the overpowering tiredness and the aching limbs, sleep came only in short bursts, a few minutes at a time,

The sky was starting to brighten with the approach of dawn when he finally gave up any hope of genuine rest and set off on the next stage of his journey.

Forcing himself forward up a long, grassy slope, he eventually reached the top and spotted the small cabin deep in the valley. The plume of smoke rising from the cabin's chimney was evidence that, even at this early hour, the owner was up and about.

Chickens roamed around the wooden cabin and over on the eastern side was a corral with five, maybe six horses. A buckboard stood beside the fence and beyond that was a small barn, a well and a broken down cart.

Matt crouched behind a boulder, giving himself time to regain his breath and consider his next move. Dressed as he was in his torn and stained prison rags, he could hardly walk casually down the slope, knock on the door and ask for food and drink and a change of clothes.

He would have to bide his time.

An hour or more passed before the cabin door opened and a figure emerged out of the shadows and into the morning sunlight. Matt shaded his eyes but he was too far away to make out any details. Except for one – it was a young woman wearing a check shirt and green pants. She crossed to the corral and led out a horse, hitching it to the buckboard before going back into the cabin.

Eventually, she reappeared, climbed aboard the wagon and swung the horse towards the dirt track that led away from the cabin. Matt waited until she was well out of sight before making his way down into the valley.

As he approached the cabin he spotted a handwritten

sign on the gate of the corral: DAWSON'S FARM.

Apart from the chickens and a few cows in a nearby meadow there were no other signs of life and he walked confidently up the step on to the boards surrounding the small house.

Cautiously, he nudged the door open and peered inside. It was a small, neatly furnished room with four chairs around a table, a stove in the corner, a chimney on the far wall and a row of cupboards over to his left. There was also a rocking chair – and it was occupied by an old man who was staring straight at him.

'Jemma? Is that you? What you forgotten this time?'

Brogan stood still and silent.

'Jemma?'

Again Matt said nothing.

'Who? Who's there?'

Slowly, stealthily, Matt moved inside the room until he was standing directly in front of the old man.

It was then that he realized it . . . the man was blind.

'I'm sorry, mister,' he said, trying to sound as friendly as possible. 'I'm just a stranger passing through.'

The man in the chair relaxed and smiled. This was the voice of an honest young man.

'Come on in, stranger. My daughter's not here but she will be back from town within the hour. Take a seat. We don't get too many strangers around here 'cept when the stage stops by.

'Where are you from and where are you headed? On your way to Broxville?'

Max listened while the old man took the chance to pump him with questions but all the time his mind was elsewhere and his eyes were searching the small room for clothes, food – anything he could take before the woman came back.

'Hope you don't mind me saying so, young feller, but I reckon you may have been on the trail a long time.'

That old man's words stunned Matt back to the present.

'What makes you think that?'

The old man chuckled. 'The thing is, son, when you don't have eyes to use you get to do other things better. Your voice is like a croak, as though you ain't had a drink for some time. And there's another thing. . . .' He chuckled again. 'My eyes may not be working but there's nothing wrong with my nose. You smell real bad, son, as though you've been sleeping in a barn these last few nights.'

Matt relaxed and allowed himself a smile.

'You're not far wrong, mister. It's been some time since I slept in a proper bed. And you are right about another thing. I've come a long way.'

'Sorry if you think I'm asking too many questions, son, but, like I said, we don't get too many visitors around here and my Jemma isn't exactly big on conversation other than chickens and her darn horses.

'As for that no-good husband of hers. . . .'

'Your daughter's married then, Mister—'

'Dawson's the name. Sam Dawson. Sure, she's married, poor girl. She and her husband, Kurt Brand, run this place for me ever since I lost my sight.' He chuckled but without humour.

'Leastways they are supposed to but he spends more time in town than he does out here. That's where she's gone now to bring him home. I 'spect she'll find him sleeping it off in some bar after a night drinking and gambling. White Horse Saloon most prob'ly.'

He sounded bitter and Brogan set about his search for a change of clothes, money, even a gun and bullets, when he was caught off guard by the man in the rocking chair.

'I didn't catch your name, son, unless maybe you didn't throw it.'

'Oh, yeah,' Brogan said eventually. 'Name's Jack Duggan.'

'Well, Mr Jack Duggan, if you'd like to pour us both a cup of coffee from that pot Jemma's left on the stove I'd be grateful.'

'Sure.'

Brogan knew he had little time to spare. He could not wait around for the daughter and her husband to get back from town. Somewhere in the house there would be shirts, pants and boots, and no self-respecting gambler would live in such a remote farm without some ready-loaded weapon handy to face unwelcome visitors. Men like Matt Brogan.

He walked across to the stove and started to fill two mugs.

Then, he paused.

'Sorry, Mr Dawson, looks like you've drunk all the coffee your daughter left,' he lied. 'Want me to make some more?'

The man did not reply straight away. Then, as if shaking off some distraction, he said: 'Sure, boil some water on the fire.'

Brogan had to hurry. Rifling through a trunk in the adjoining bedroom, he pulled out a black shirt and a pair of pants. At the side of the bed was a pair of leather boots.

He stripped off his prison rags and pulled on the clothes, which fitted a lot better than he could have hoped.

He searched through a couple of drawers and was about to give up finding anything else that was useful when he spotted it; a small door at the side of the bed.

Inside, he found what he was looking for – and a whole lot more. A gun, holster, a rifle and a stash of dollar bills. Brogan rammed his shirt pocket full of money, strapped on the holster and checked the New Army Model Colt, a remnant of the hundreds of thousands used in the War Between the States.

As he got to his feet he turned to see Sam Dawson standing in the doorway. For a brief, worrying moment he thought he had been mistaken about the old man's lack of sight. He was pointing a rifle directly at him.

'You hadn't ought to be in here, Jack. This is my daughter's room. And Kurt's, of course. Even I ain't allowed in here.'

'Sorry, Mr Dawson.' He tried to make the apology sound genuine. 'I was just looking for a pot to fill so that I could make some fresh coffee. I guess I wandered in here by mistake.'

Sam Dawson remained unimpressed. 'Never once got a bedroom mixed up with a kitchen, even after I got myself blinded.'

Matt made a move for the door.

The old man stiffened and tightened his grip on the rifle.

'I think I told you what it's like when you can't see like other folk. The rest of your senses get a boost. Like how I smelt you because I got a stronger nose sense. Well, hearing's the same. I know exactly where you are in the room so if you think I would miss you if I let off a couple of shots with this here scatter gun you are sure entitled to try your luck.'

'Look, Mr Dawson, I. . . .'

'I misjudged you, Duggan. You sounded like an honest young feller but you aren't are you? The thing is – I haven't touched that pot since Jemma put it there. It's still full of coffee. So the least you are is a liar, Jack Duggan, if that is your name. What else are you? If you're just a small-time thief I suggest you get on your way. There's nothing here worth stealing.'

An awkward silence followed before the old man said: 'So, what's it to be? Do we stand here till my daughter and her husband get home or are you going to be on your way?'

Brogan agreed. An escaped prisoner no doubt with a heavy price on his head could not afford to hang around too long, especially in stolen clothes, wearing a stolen gun and preparing to steal a saddle and horse.

'You're right, Mr Dawson – Sam. But I mean you no harm. That's the God's honest truth. And I don't doubt for a minute that if you squeeze that trigger it would make a mess of me as well as your daughter's bedroom.

'I just ask you to trust those first instincts and step aside to let me on my way.'

He scooped up the discarded prison clothes.

'I want you to thank your daughter and her husband for me and tell them I'll be back to say it personally as soon as I can.'

The old man frowned. 'Thank them? What for?'

'They'll know, Sam, trust me.' The man lowered his rifle and felt Brogan brush past him. As he reached the door, he turned.

'Be seeing you soon, Sam. And that's a promise,' he said and headed for the corral.

Choosing the pick of four horses, he lifted a saddle off the fence and prepared to head south, avoiding the town of Broxville and the danger of bumping into the Brands on their way home.

He left Arizona Territory and entered New Mexico the following morning. The town of Alvorado was still a two-day ride away. At least two days before he came face to face with the men he had vowed to kill . . . three men who, three years ago, had taken away all he loved in the world and destroyed his life.

Three years ago. . . .

CHAPTER THREE

Three years ago. . . .

Katie Brogan shouted across the small yard to her son.

'Toby! Come in, now. Supper's ready!'

Nine-year-old Toby Brogan threw the ball for his dog Skip to chase – Skip never tired of chasing things, especially rabbits – and turned to run towards the house. His pa wasn't home yet; probably wouldn't be back until tomorrow but that didn't matter, it just meant a bigger share of the meat pie for him. And a bit more for him to sneak under the table for Skip.

Skip, ball in mouth, trotted alongside him like every faithful dog should do and they had just reached the yard gate when Toby spotted them in the distance. Three riders.

'Visitors, ma!' he shouted. 'Friends of Pa, maybe.'

Katie Brogan came back out of the house and stood on the porch, peering into the distance and the setting sun. She didn't want visitors, not when Matt was away.

'Go inside, Toby, your supper's on the table. It's your favourite.'

She ruffled the boy's hair as he went by and reminded him that Skip had his own food in his own place. It was a smiling reminder but she was not feeling as playful as she sounded as Toby ran into the house, followed by his faithful dog.

Matt should have been back by now. Two days, he had said, that's how long he would be away. But now it was nearing the end of the third and he was still not home.

There had been times, a dozen years back, when preacher's daughter Katie Miller and young deputy sheriff Matthew Brogan were courting when he was often away for long days and nights.

She understood that. It was all part of a lawman's job. But those days were behind them. Five years ago, Matt handed in his badge and the couple along with their young son had settled down to their life on a small farm. Katie had never been happier, freed of the fear that her husband would be gunned down by some young trigger-happy drunk leaving a saloon.

A man with a star was always a target for a kid wanting to make a reputation for himself but nobody was interested in a small-time farmer.

There were still times when Matt was away on business but those occasions were rare and were always for the betterment of life on the farm.

Despite young Toby's suggestion that the approaching riders might be friends of her husband, Katie knew differently. Since leaving the sheriff's office, Matt's only friends had been those he made in town and the approaching trio were not coming from there. Whoever they were, they were no friends of Matt Brogan.

She stood on the porch and waited for the horsemen to reach the yard. There was no cause to worry about the appearance of three strangers – the Brogan spread was barely a mile off the main cross-country route – and she couldn't explain the feeling of nervousness as they pulled their horses to a halt a few feet away from the house.

'Evenin' ma'am.' It was the big red-faced man with a bushy beard, the oldest of the trio, who spoke. He leaned forward on the horn of his saddle and smiled. 'We saw the smoke from your house and wondered if you could spare a few canteens of water. Me and the boys have ridden a long way. We'd sure be grateful.'

Katie Brogan studied the three strangers. The speaker was a thick-set man in his sixties with long unkempt hair spattered with streaks of grey to match the beard. He was dressed in all black, except for a white band around his hat. The one on his left was a thinner, younger version but clearly hewn from the same block. Mid-twenties, Katie guessed. The third man was not a smiler. His dark, Hispanic features were set firm. He was neither handsome nor ugly but his deep blue eyes emphasized his cold stare.

'Help yourselves,' she told them. 'There's a trough over there for your horses and you can fill your canteens from the well. I've got to get inside and give my son his supper. My husband will be home soon and he'll be expecting to have his meal ready.'

The big man lifted his hat by way of thanks and the trio dismounted as Katie went back into the house.

The men watered their horses and refilled their canteens and, that done, the old man perched on the wall of the well and lit himself a cheroot. He looked at the small layout surrounding the house.

A few cattle were scattered around the grazing land beyond the corral. There was a pile of chopped wood near a barn.

The man finished his cheroot and crushed the stub into the dust.

'D'you know, boys, I'm feeling real hungry after our long ride. And you heard the lady; there ain't no man around to enjoy her cooking. Reckon she might be happy if we obliged. You know, show her how she's appreciated.'

The thin one grinned.

'Pretty lady, too, Pa,' he said. The non-smiler grunted and the big man chuckled, slapping the other on the back.

'Ain't nothing wrong with your eyesight, son. Reckon the little lady may take a shine to you. Let's go inside and see.'

'She said her husband would be home soon, Pa,' the son protested but his father laughed again.

'Which means he ain't home right now. Time enough for you to work your charms on the lady.'

The son grinned, ran his fingers through his long, untidy hair and followed the others into the house.

Without knocking, the old man pushed open the door and entered the room. The boy was sitting at the table eating his supper of pie and potatoes. His mother stood at a stove in the corner.

'Smells good,' the old man said.

'Looks good too, Pa, and I ain't talking about the pie.'

Katie stiffened, frightened by the sneering glare from the old man's son. The one with the cold eyes walked towards the table, gripped Toby by the shirt collar and pulled him away from his chair. Skip followed him and barked his own protest.

'Lose yourself, kid – and take that stinking mutt with you.' The force of his push sent the boy sprawling across the floor and he crashed into a cupboard at the foot of a flight of stairs.

Toby let out a yell of pain and Skip ran to his side to see what had happened to his young master. Katie made a move towards her stricken son but the old man grabbed her around the waist and lifted her off her feet.

'Calm yourself, lady. You don't want to see your boy getting hurt, do you? Why don't you just sit here while me and the boys enjoy some of that meat pie of yours. After all, water from a well and a horse trough ain't exactly what you'd call real hospitality.'

'Ma? What do they want, Ma?'

Toby's voice trembled. His mother tried to shake free but the big man tightened his vice-like grip on her.

'Go to your room, Toby,' she said, trying to keep the terror out of her voice. She knew what was going to happen but she could not let her son witness what was to come. 'These men will be on their way just as soon as they've had some supper.'

The big man grinned. 'Sure, that's right, boy. We'll be out of here before you know it.'

Toby got to his feet and started to climb the stairs. Then, turning, he spoke with a child's defiance. 'You'd best be gone before my pa gets home or else you'll be in real trouble, especially if you eat all his supper.'

The trio laughed, cold, humourless laughs that told Katie Brogan that these men would not be leaving before they had done with her. She felt sick. Where was Matthew? Why had this business that she knew nothing about taken him away for so long? What could have been so important that he had to go all the way to Denver? She felt herself praying: Please, God, let him be home soon. Let him be here before these evil men. . . .

Suddenly the one who had called the big man Pa got to his feet.

'I guess there must be some drinks around here somewhere,' he said, pulling open some cupboard doors and dragging out the contents, scattering them across the floor. Then – a yell of triumph. He reached deep inside and pulled out two bottles of whiskey.

'Now we can have some real fun. What do you say, lady? You would like to have some fun wouldn't you?'

Using his teeth to pull out the stopper from one of the bottles, sliding the other across the table, he reached out and grabbed Kate's wrist, pulling her from his father's grasp. She tried to shake herself free but the young man, despite his slender frame, was much too strong.

'Leave me alone!' she pleaded. 'Please! Leave us be!'

The man laughed, an ugly throaty sound.

'Aw, that's not very friendly, is it? Here, have a drink.' He tried to force the bottle between her lips but she turned her head away and the whiskey poured down her chin and on to the front of her dress.

'Now, look see what you've done. Spilled all that good whiskey down your front. I suppose you expect me to lick it off now.' He took a long swig from the bottle.

'Please,' Katie begged again, this time tears flowing. 'Why can't you leave me alone?'

The man turned away. 'Hear that, Pa? Hear what she says and there was you telling me how much she would like me. She just ain't being pleasant at all.'

The old man snatched up the second bottle, pulled off the stopper and took a long drink before getting to his feet.

'Then maybe you need me to show you how it's done, boy.' He pushed his son to one side but as Katie cowered away he simply smiled and said: 'There's no place to go, lady.'

He grabbed her by the hair, pulled her towards him and, his face twisted in a threatening lecherous leer, pressed his mouth over hers.

She wanted to vomit. Her whole world was falling apart, her husband was not here to save her from this disgusting creature who was about to brutalize her.

She tried to fight him off when he pushed her to the floor and he was on top of her, ripping her clothes, urged on by the others' laughter and cheers.

But suddenly he stopped – halted by the shout from the top of the staircase. The man ran his arm through the whiskey-drenched whiskers and got to his feet.

'Well now, young fella, what have we got here?'

The others followed the big man's gaze towards the top of the stairs. Toby, with Skip at his ankles, was pointing a rifle in his direction.

'You leave my mother alone, mister!' he yelled. 'Just you let her be!'

The man laughed. 'Now, son, you ain't gonna. . . .'

He didn't finish. Panicked by the sight of his mother being attacked, Toby squeezed hard on the trigger of the rifle. The recoil sent him toppling backwards and the bullet flew harmlessly overhead and shattered the mirror above the fire grate.

But it also cost the frightened nine-year-old his life. Spinning round and without a thought, the old man's son fired his six-gun in the direction of the rifle shot. Not once – but twice. The first bullet ripped into Toby's stomach; the second hitting him full in the chest. He was dead before his frail body tumbled halfway down the staircase.

Katie screamed and pulled herself free of the old man's grasp. She raced across the room. Throwing herself on to her son, as though she believed she could protect him from further harm. Screaming ever louder she cradled her dead son in her arms.

'He could have killed you, Pa. The kid could have killed you.'

Nobody was listening to the feeble bleating of the young gunman. The old man slid into a chair. This wasn't part of the plan. Sure, he was aiming to have some fun with the woman, a few drinks and they would be on their way. Nobody was supposed to get hurt or killed. The gun crazy son of his. Damn fool! The kid couldn't have hit a barn door with that rifle.

His thoughts were interrupted by another scream from the woman.

'You killed him! You killed my son!' she yelled.

He turned in time to see that the woman had picked up the rifle and was pointing it at his chest. But, just like with her son, the act cost Katie Brogan her life. This time it was the third man, the one with the cold, staring eyes, who spotted the danger and did not hesitate. He fired twice and the woman fell on top of her dead son.

He looked across at the old man.

'That's twice, Mr McLagan,' he said, reholstering his gun. 'Two lives wasted because you and Roy had to have your fun.'

Alex McLagan took another long drink from the whiskey bottle and glared at the man who had just killed the boy's mother.

'When did you get yourself a conscience, Mex?'

He stared at the two bodies at the foot of the staircase.

'You're right, though, she was a waste. Pity about the kid, too.'

He threw down the empty bottle, picked his hat off the table and headed for the door. But it was the Mexican who reached it first and, as he pulled it open, he spotted the approaching rider, silhouetted high on the hillside against the deep red of the early night sky.

Matt Brogan was tired. It had been a long ride and he was already late. Katie would be worried and young Toby would be eager to see him back – if only for the candy bars he would be bringing from the trip to Denver.

But candy was not all he would be bringing home this time. The business trip had gone even better than he had hoped. He had kept his plans secret from his wife and son for long enough but now was the time to tell her everything.

In a few days Katie and Toby would get their wish – to move out of the isolated farmhouse, out of Colorado and into Junction City, Kansas. Although only a small town of fewer than 3,000 inhabitants in Katie's home state, Junction City was the perfect place for the Brogan family to set up their general store and ladies' emporium. He had managed to keep his plans to sell the farm a secret from his wife and son but now the papers had been signed and the money was being transferred into a Kansas State Bank. Thanks to the new owners of the Brogan farm and pastures, it was time to celebrate.

It would be the perfect birthday present for the woman in his life.

He pushed his horse even harder. Night was falling fast and soon Toby and his mother would be sitting down to their supper and then it would be time for bed for his son. Matt had to get home before that.

He gave his tiring horse an extra nudge as he reached the brow of the hill. Once at the top he paused, leaning forward to gaze into the valley below at the place that they had called home for much of their married life but that they were about to leave behind. An isolated farm almost ten miles from the nearest town was no place to bring up a boy like Toby. He needed friends, proper schooling – though Katie did her best – and a chance to see that there was more to life than chickens and cattle.

True, the farm had been the start of a new life for them, a chance for Matt to put away his guns and sheriff's star.

He had managed to keep his northern sympathies in check throughout the four-year conflict but when Abraham Lincoln was assassinated by some disaffected young actor only days after peace broke out he realized that the tales of hostility and hatred still festered and in many cases flourished in certain parts of what were supposed to be the new United States.

Neighbouring New Mexico was full of disillusioned southerners still determined to live by the bullet rather than accept the peace deal of a genuine Union.

At the beginning of the war Matt had needed little persuasion to follow his wife's pleas and put the future of their young son at the top of his list of priorities. In the two years since Robert E Lee had signed the south's surrender at Appomattox he had worked and saved to secure that future.

The time had come. Now, as he sat astride his horse and looked down through the gathering gloom at his small farmhouse he spotted the three horses, saddled and tethered to a hitching post.

'Looks like we've got visitors, boy,' he said, patting his horse. 'Hope they've left a hungry man some supper.'

He dug his heels into the reluctant horse's ribs and they headed down the slope towards the house – just a few more strides that would lead to the discovery that would change his life forever.

It was the moment he entered his home and was beaten unconscious from behind as he stared in horror at the bodies of his wife and son slumped at the foot of the stairs.

Matthew Brogan stood in the makeshift dock and listened to the circuit judge summing up a double murder case.

Judge Henry Coburn was tired. He had travelled halfway across the territory and this was his third major case in four days. Neither of the others had been easy – not like this one where the evidence was clear-cut. Brogan had killed his wife and child when she discovered that he was planning to move out of the territory and into Kansas.

Maybe he hadn't planned the killing but that was often the way.

He coughed, took a drink from the water glass and said: 'I have heard the evidence of the three witnesses of how they called at the Brogan farm in search of water for their horses and to their horror found the prisoner standing outside the blazing farmhouse, rifle in one hand and a near empty whiskey bottle in the other and cursing about treachery and deceit and how he had killed both of them in a fit of rage.

'Having listened to many residents of the town speaking out on behalf of Brogan, I was reluctant to believe that a man liked by many people could perform such a despicable act – especially against a child not yet ten years of age – but kind words are not evidence. So I had your sheriff investigate the witnesses' credibility. He reported that the three men – Alex McLagan, his son Roy and the Mexican Juan Herrera are respected citizens and ranch owners in New Mexico.

'They had nothing whatever to gain from bringing the prisoner into town when if, as the prisoner claimed, they were the guilty parties. They could simply have ridden away and left the territory without anybody in town knowing they had even been here. Instead they behaved like upright citizens, which leads me to believe that they are speaking the truth.'

Matt had stared across the courtroom at the men who had dragged him into town to testify against him. The old man, hair trimmed, beard shaven and dressed in a business suit, had the appearance of a respectable ranch owner; likewise his son; only the Mexican, dressed in black, looked what he was – a hired gun.

The judge's words drifted back. . . .

'They had been travelling home from a cattlemen's convention and were unfortunate to come across such a scene. Sadly, they were too late to save Mrs Brogan and her young son.

'I have considered the prisoner's claim that it was the three men who had killed his wife and child, but he can give no reason, nor can he explain why, if they are the real culprits, they did not also kill him and ride off into the night. Instead they acted like the good citizens your sheriff has discovered them to be and went out of their way to bring Matthew Brogan into town to face the charge of murder.

'The prisoner also admits that he was planning to sell his farm and move to Kansas yet also says his wife and son were told nothing of this.

'It is the verdict of this court that Matthew Brogan killed both Katherine and Toby Brogan in a drunken rage, probably brought on when he told them of his plans to sell their home and they had refused to agree to the move.

'We have learned that he went to Denver and completed the sale – again pointing to the fact that Brogan was behaving unreasonably.'

Matt stared into the faces of the three men who had killed his family, beaten him senseless and dragged him into town for the trial. Their eyes were cold, their faces expressionless, showing no emotion. Yet he knew that, inwardly, they were gloating, sneering at him. They were killers, all of them. It did not matter who had carried out the butchery, they were all guilty and one day they would pay. As God was his judge he vowed he would have vengeance.

It was then that he heard the words of condemnation.

'This court believes that, although death by hanging is the appropriate sentence for such a hideous crime,

Matthew Brogan does not deserve such an easy, sympathetic end to his life. I therefore pronounce that the prisoner will be escorted to a penitentiary where he will serve fifteen years of hard labour with no remission.'

Those were the last words he heard before he was dragged away to the cell to await transportation to the penitentiary that was due to be his home for the next fifteen years.

He was still in his cramped jail cell when Judge Henry Coburn boarded the Santa Fe-bound stage, $3,000 richer thanks to Alex McLagan's generosity. The old man was well aware that there were times when one good turn deserved another.

CHAPTER FOUR

Matt Brogan woke suddenly in a cold sweat. The nightmare was still with him, still haunting him after three years. The recurring horrors of how he stood helpless and hog-tied as the three men dragged the bodies from the house, set fire to his home and then, after shooting the yapping dog Skip, forced him into town to face trial for murder.

The old man even enjoyed telling him what they had planned. They had kept him alive to get him convicted so that they could ride away without fear of being followed by lawmen or bounty hunters. Case solved.

He had stared into their eyes while the judge delivered his sentence and he still saw them in his dreams. They were faces he would never forget.

Now, three years later, he was reliving the hell of it all.

Suddenly, he realized that it was not just the nightmare that had shaken him out of his sleep. He had heard something – a movement in the bushes. A coyote, maybe. Or a bobcat.

After his long day's ride he had settled down in a remote clearing hoping for a few hours' rest before continuing his journey.

Cautiously, he stretched out for his gun-belt, just out of reach, but he never quite made it.

'Easy, man, you won't be needing that.'

A figure, dressed in a grey shirt, black pants and hat, stepped out of the shadows. He was pointing a gun at Matt's chest. Matt reckoned that the stranger was in his mid-thirties. Brogan withdrew his hand.

'That's better,' the newcomer grinned and put his gun back in its holster. 'I saw the glow from your dying fire and thought there might be a coffee pot that's still warm. The name's Jed, by the way.'

'Just Jed?'

The man smiled. 'For now.'

'Jack Duggan,' Matt said, pushing himself up on to his elbow. 'Coffee's gone cold, I expect, but you're welcome to make us another.'

'My pleasure,' the stranger said pleasantly.

'You're out riding late,' Matt said by way of conversation as the two men sat in front of the recharged fire.

Jed cupped his mug, took another drink of his coffee and said: 'Goes with the job.' He added nothing extra and Matt decided that his new companion did not want to say any more so he let the matter rest.

'You headed anywhere special, Jack?'

Matt shrugged. 'Got some business down in New Mexico. Some men I've got to see. How about you?'

'Same,' Jed said, throwing away the dregs of the coffee mug and getting to his feet. Then, to Matt's surprise, he stretched out his arm in a move to shake hands.

'Thanks for the coffee, Jack. Guess I'll let you get back to some sleep and I'll be on my way. If we bump into each other again I'll owe you a beer.'

'New Mexico's a big place but I'll hold you to that,' Matt said, taking the outstretched hand. He stood and watched the other man as he untied his horse from the bush, mounted up and rode off into the night.

Alone again, he settled down to try to make up some of

that lost sleep. But his mind was elsewhere. It was down in Alvorado, the small valley town some forty miles out of Santa Fe. McLagan and son and the Mexican may, as the judge had said, be upright citizens and landowners but that said more for the law around Alvorado than it did of the three men. It changed nothing. They had killed his wife and had convinced a judge and jury that they were passing strangers who had only done their duty by bringing a culprit to court.

Shortly before dawn after a couple of hours of interrupted sleep, Matt Brogan saddled up and set off on the last leg of his search for revenge.

CHAPTER FIVE

Quince Leroy was the sheriff of Alvorado but his job had nothing to do with enforcing law and order in the town. There was none.

The paymaster of Leroy, and everybody else within miles of the town was Alex McLagan, banker, landlord and the biggest ranch owner in the territory. Leroy's deputy was one of the McLagan boys, his youngest son, Lance; another – Roy – ran the saloon and casino. The mayor was Abe Jackson, the McLagan family mouthpiece.

Alvorado was a McLagan town.

Leroy sat at his desk and studied the poster that had been delivered to his office a few days earlier.

WANTED for BANK ROBBERY
$2,000 REWARD
MAX BENSON

Below the wording was a fading picture of the man standing in front of his office desk.

'Two thousand dollars, huh? You must have some important friends, mister.'

The man said nothing. He knew exactly what Leroy was getting at. Nobody found protection in Alvorado without the cash to pay McLagan. And Leroy was the man who stood between this man Benson and the say-so of McLagan.

Benson reached inside his shirt pocket and withdrew a wad of notes, which he threw on to the desk. Leroy counted them carefully before sliding them into a drawer.

'Five hundred. I think that will keep the law out of your hair for a few weeks.'

Benson grunted but said nothing and left the office to head for the nearest saloon. He knew the saloons well. This was not his first visit to Alvorado. It had been less than a year since the last time when he was on the run from Texas. But five hundred bucks was a small price to pay for the security McLagan and his men offered. And he still had the best part of $8,000 in his saddle-bag, the rewards of the bank robbery up in Missouri that had led to the issue of the wanted poster bearing his name.

'One of these days, Leroy,' he muttered to himself, 'one of these days you ain't goin' to feel so smug.'

Back at the office Quince Leroy got to his feet, walked over to the window and watched one of his more generous customers cross the street and mount the steps into The Diamond Bar to put more of his money into the pockets of the McLagan family.

He chuckled. There was nowhere that the McLagans had not got their claws into. If Alex McLagan did not own a place – general stores were of no interest – they still had to pay into his protection plan. Insurance, he called it. Insurance against fire and damage, caused, naturally enough, by members of the McLagan spread.

'It takes hard money to pay lookouts to man the pass into town,' he had told Leroy often enough, 'so let's call them deputy sheriffs. Anybody riding into Alvorado from the north does not come for the pleasure of your company, Quince. They want to be sure that half of the lawmen from Texas to Montana ain't just going to walk in here and drag them off. If they want to put holes in each other once they get here that's their business. All you have to do is clear up the mess they'll leave behind, and they'll have put in enough money to pay their funeral bills.'

The arrangement suited Leroy perfectly. He had done his life's share of good work as a grey jacket in the Civil War and where had that got him? A bullet in the leg had left him with a limp and memories of his part in a rampaging raid on a town of innocents.

And where else could he pick up more than $500 a month for collecting protection fees from men who, not so long ago, he would gladly have seen dangling from the end of a rope. All in the name of law and order.

But Quince Leroy had discovered that there were no rewards for wounded war heroes, especially those from the losing side. He had learned that every man has his price and Alex McLagan was ready to take advantage of that.

He set alight the wanted poster bearing Benson's picture. In the unlikely event of a lawman or bounty hunter breaking through the guard that McLagan had placed on the hillsides three miles out of town there would be no evidence to say that the sheriff of Alvorado was even aware of the man on the run.

That was the way he liked it these days. No evidence.

Sinking into his chair, the bogus lawman prepared for another routine day in the lives and deaths of the town built in Hell.

By midday the sun's rays forced Matt Brogan to seek shelter in brush close to a stream. He stripped to his waist, knelt on the bank and splashed himself in the cooling waters.

He reckoned that he was still more than an hour's ride from the town of Alvorado but he had still not made any definite plans of how he was going to finish the job he had set himself.

He learned at his trial that the McLagans were important people in these parts but he knew them only as brutal killers. Three years in the penitentiary had not been wasted in feeling sorry for himself.

Instead he had made use of the few chances he got to learn about the McLagan clan. Alex, the old man and owner of the Big L ranch, was known as The Protector.

'The law won't get you unless Alex McLagan says so,' was always the message. You would pay a high price for his protection – he uses some of the money to pay off greedy lawmen who would rather take easy cash than work to drag wanted men back for trial or reward.

'And if he takes you on as a cowhand the pay wouldn't be enough to make a flea fat,' he was told. 'You'll always owe Alex McLagan from the minute you arrive until they throw the last sod on your coffin.'

Matt Brogan was determined to change all that.

Brogan had been told often that he would not be able to ride straight into the town of Alvorado, so when he spotted the two men high on the hillside at the head of the canyon he knew what was expected.

He dismounted, unbuckled his holster and hooked it over the horn of his saddle. Then he stepped away from his horse and raised his arms above his head as a sign to the two lookouts that he wanted to talk. He waited.

Minutes passed before a figure emerged from the mouth of the canyon – a big, barrel-chested man with a full black beard carrying a rifle at his side. There was a low-hung gun-belt on his left hip.

Matt waited until he was a few feet away and then tried a friendly smile. It didn't work.

The man kept his rifle pointed at Brogan's chest.

'Where you planning on heading, mister?'

'The name's Duggan,' Matt said. 'Jack Duggan.'

'I didn't ask your name. I asked where you're headed?'

The man was under orders and he knew how to obey them.

Matt knew he would get nowhere by drawing the man into a confrontation.

'Alvorado's along this road, isn't it? And Alex McLagan's place?'

Then it came – the moment Matt had feared since he set out on this revenge mission; the arrival of one of the men who might remember him. Sure, he had changed a lot since the trial. He was leaner, darker with none of the good looks that had attracted Katie when they were younger. Three years in prison had destroyed what was left of his youthful appearance.

But now came the real test. The rider approaching from the gap in the hillside was the Mexican who had been there for the killing of his wife and son. If Matt was recognized he was about to enter the final moments of his life. His gun and holster, which he had surrendered as a sign of goodwill towards the hillside lookouts, were still hanging on his saddle-horn. Now all he could do was pray that the Mexican had forgotten he had ever seen him.

The man dismounted and walked over, a swaggering stride, his thumbs inside his belt, his hat pushed towards the back of his head. His steel blue eyes as cold as Matt remembered. He hated the Mexican all over again.

'We got another one, Mitch?'

The big man who had met Matt answered: 'Says his name's Duggan. Looking for the Big L. Says he knows Alex.'

'Whoa!' Matt stepped in. 'I didn't say I know him. I'd heard about him and I've been told he looks out for men like me . . . men the law would like to see at the end of a rope.'

It was a gamble. If the Mexican saw through this he was a dead man and no mistake.

'Who did you kill, Mister Duggan. Some sheriff maybe? Or some bluebelly's lady? Ha! Ha!'

Matt felt himself sigh so loud he thought the others might even have heard it. The Mexican's questions were confirmation that he had no memory of the man he had sent to prison.

'Nobody,' Matt said, 'cept maybe a railroad man who got shot up.'

'A train robber, eh? Who you been riding with?'

Matt didn't answer at once. How much did the Mexican know about various gangs? The Youngers, the James boys? It was time to take another chance.

'The Reno brothers. I was there when the gang robbed the Ohio and Mississippi Railroad up in Seymour, Indiana, in sixty-six. And I was there when some vigilantes hung some of the gang in sixty-eight.'

'You got away.'

Matt grinned. 'Seems like it. I'm here to prove it.'

'So – you got money? You can pay?'

'Sure I can pay, but not till I see what I'm getting for my money.'

The Mexican sneered.

'You don't make the rules, *señor*. We do.'

Matt returned the sneer.

'And here was me thinking that Alex McLagan called the shots around these parts. Well, I guess I'll just turn right round and be on my way.'

It was another gamble. The Mexican had believed the tale about riding with Frank and John Reno, and that had been a bigger risk. Again his gamble worked.

The man with the black beard stepped forward.

'Hold it right there, Duggan.' He turned to face the Mexican. 'Alex ain't gonna be too happy if we turn good money away. If this guy ain't who he said he is, well – Alex can solve that problem, easy enough.'

'The boss don't know he is here. We could just kill him, take his money. Alex never know.'

Mitch snorted.

'Ain't you the one, Mex? Testing me out like that. Well, I ain't no fish waiting to be hooked that easy. We both know that Brad is still up there in the hills watching everything. What story would you pay him to tell his uncle if we do what you say?'

The Mexican spread his arms wide and let out a loud guffaw.

'Mitch! *Amigo*! You are right. I joke.'

He turned to Matt. 'Alvorado is three miles down this road. You call in at the office of the sheriff and he will take your money. His name is Quince Leroy. And remember, *señor* Duggan, there is only one road in and out of the town. You leave when Mister McLagan says so. You understand?'

'Clear enough,' Matt said. 'It sounds like the place I have just left.'

Matt strapped on his gun-belt, remounted and led his horse on a slow walk towards the canyon road that led to the town of Alvorado and the showdown with the men who had slaughtered his family.

Their lives, as well as his own, meant nothing to him. Matt Brogan knew he was walking in dead man's boots.

Amy Bannon felt the wheel of her buggy begin to shake under her. Roy had been promising to fix it for more than a week but, like most other things he had promised, he had never got round to it.

Like their wedding. Three times they had arranged for the preacher to be at the ranch and each time Roy had found reasons to be out on the road. It was not that he did not love her or did not want to marry her, she really believed that, but when Alex McLagan called, his eldest son had to answer.

And Alex was calling a lot more often recently. The old man was not in the best of health. He had developed a deep-throated cough that came in regular fits, confining him to his bed for several days at a time. His sight was failing and he could no longer ride the open range to keep a personal watch over the Big L operation.

He needed more cowhands, more men he could trust, and they were hard to find around Alvorado.

Amy pulled the buggy to a halt just as the wheel gave away completely. She had reached the small, sheltered lake on the northern fringe of the McLagan spread, well out of the range of the cowhands or any other prying eyes.

Picnicking alone was no fun but it was better than sitting around the house killing time until her fiancé decided to put in an appearance

But this was her favourite spot in the whole of the New Mexico Territory. Here she could sunbathe and swim undisturbed.

She climbed down from the buggy, gave a quick examination of the damaged wheel and shrugged. It was a long walk back to her small house where she lived with her father but that was for later.

She spread her rug out on the grass and stretched out, her face to the blazing sun, her eyes closed against the glare.

This would be bliss, she thought, if only Roy was lying at her side.

Where was he now? At which far off corner of the vast McLagan empire was he driving men to even more fence building, cattle branding or whatever cowboys did to earn money?

It was strange that he never confided in her, never told her even the most basic issues of work on a ranch. How could she be expected to become a ranch owner's wife without his help?

There were times when Amy wondered what life would have been like if her mother had lived through the fever that had taken her when Amy was only 12 years old. Would they have gone back east – to Chicago maybe, where she could have been properly schooled and met other young people? What if her father had accepted the McLagans' offer for the farm when her brother Tommy went off to fight in the war, never to return?

Life would have been so different and there would have been other young men in her life, not just Roy McLagan. But all that was in the past and she was still thinking about Roy when she felt the sudden change . . . a shadow fell across her face. She opened her eyes to find herself staring up into the silhouetted figure of a man.

Startled, she lifted herself into a sitting position and shielded her eyes against the sunlight.

'Sorry to disturb you, miss. I was riding past and I spotted the buggy with the broken wheel and figured you might need some help.'

The voice was quiet, polite and pleasant – a combination that Amy had not heard in a long time. She got to her feet and stood in front of the stranger. He was tall, rangy, fadingly handsome but, like most of the men she knew, could have improved his appearance with a shave. He also had a pleasant smile.

'Did I startle you? Sorry again.'

Amy returned the smile.

'I was just daydreaming. I was hoping that you might be my fiancé, I'm expecting him to fix that wheel when he comes by.'

It was a lie but it served a purpose. As pleasant as this stranger looked and sounded, she did not want him to think that she would be alone for long.

'More apologies from me, then,' the man said, 'for not being him, I mean. I'll just fill up my canteen and be on my way.'

Amy stood and watched the stranger as he crouched at the water's edge. Suddenly she said: 'My name's Amy Bannon.'

The man finished filling his canteen, took a long drink before coming towards her.

'Jack Duggan,' Matt said. 'Pleased to meet you, Miss Bannon.' He touched the brim of his hat.

They chatted for a while, exchanging pleasantries, but the appearance of a dark cloud over the distant hills threatened to ruin the rest of the afternoon. And there was still no sign of the missing fiancé.

'Looks like a storm is on its way,' Matt said as the sun disappeared behind the clouds. 'If you don't want to wait for your man I'll take a look at that wheel.'

'Thanks, I'd be grateful. It seems like Roy has been held up at the ranch. His father works him much too hard.'

'Roy?'

'He's my fiancé, Roy McLagan.'

Matt said nothing. He fixed the wheel but he worked in silence.

A dozen miles away, beyond the western fringe of the Big L, Roy McLagan was not mending fences or pushing his men to work even harder. Ranch business was a long way from his thoughts.

He was drinking in a remote cantina with a Mexican girl on his lap and a poker hand in his fist.

Across the table, three of the Big L's cowhands made up the card game but Roy's mind was not on poker. Cards weren't fun. Girls, especially girls like Jacquinta, plump, Mexican and eager. They were fun.

Amy Bannon was also a long way from his mind. Some day – any day would be too soon for him and could come even earlier than he cared to think if the old man got his way – he would marry the girl and cut down on his visits to the cantina. He smiled at that thought. Cut down – maybe to three visits a week instead of five.

There was more to life than a doting wife and looking after cattle. Roy McLagan had big ideas . . . bigger even than the old man's.

Sure, his father had built up the Big L out of nothing and he had trod on a few toes and paid some good money to get where he was but his eyesight was fading and his health was bad. That was not for Roy. He even chuckled to himself at the idea that the old man owned the town of Alvorado.

That belonged to him. Roy McLagan. But there was a big wide world of opportunity out there and Roy was going to have his share. His mealy-mouthed half-brother Lance could have the Big L and the stink of cattle. He could even have Amy if he wanted her. Roy had seen him going all goggle-eyed the minute she showed up at the ranch.

Women – they were ten to the dollar.

That was not the life for Roy McLagan.

Arizona Territory. That's where the action was. Riches and power beyond even his father's wildest dreams.

Soon the time would come when he would get his men around him and set out on his own private war. He would drive the small-time farmers out of their homes, he would burn their petty little homesteads to the ground and he would do more for the McLagan name than the old man had managed in twenty-five years.

Suddenly Roy threw his cards on to the table.

'Count me out, boys,' he chuckled. 'Me and Jacquinta here's gonna have some fun.' He pushed the girl off his lap, grabbed her around the waist and they dashed behind a curtain and into the room at the back of the building.

Just then, a cloudburst sent rain crashing on to the tin roof of the cantina. Roy McLagan did not notice as he ripped open the girl's clothing and forced her back on to the makeshift bed.

Amy Bannon, the Big L and Alvorado could wait. Even his big plans could wait. Roy McLagan had other things in mind.

The lone rider lowered his spyglasses and leaned forward in his saddle. He had seen all he needed to see. Two men had come down to meet the man who had said his name was Jack Duggan and after a long chat they eventually agreed to let him pass. Still high on the hillside was a third member of the group guarding the entrance to the canyon road that led to town.

The rider knew that was not the route he could take. For him there would be no way past the three guards without a gunfight and he was not ready for that. Not yet.

He had no intention of announcing his arrival to the man he was following. Instead, he turned his horse away and guided it slowly down the hillside and on to the flats that stretched barren towards the horizon.

That way he would arrive in Alvorado unannounced after darkness fell the following day.

He pulled his horse to a halt, lit himself a cheroot and

wondered not for the first time if the man he was seeking had given him a single thought in the past two years. He doubted it. After all, his brother was just another victim, another nameless notch on the gun of a killer.

He sat for several minutes deep in thought before throwing the remains of his smoke into the dust. He had waited a long time to settle the score so his patience would hold for an extra day or two. And the prospect of having an ally, however reluctant he might be, was a welcome bonus.

It was not that he had got on well with his elder brother, Shane. The two were as different as it was possible for brothers with the same parents could be. Shane was a raucous, outgoing youngster ready to pit his wits and fists against anybody large or small who challenged him. By contrast the rider was a quiet, studious type who wanted to be an attorney from the moment he knew what an attorney was.

Naturally enough, the brothers had their fights, which Shane always won, while he comforted himself with the knowledge that one day Shane would need him more than the other way round.

Shane was two years his senior and believed that entitled him to be boss of the house when their father took a bullet in the first year of the war, leaving their ailing mother alone to bring them up.

'Where's your schoolin' gonna get you now, little brother. Now that we need money it's going to be up to me.'

He had ignored the jibe because he knew that irked his brother more than he ever showed.

He could hardly believe it when Shane arrived home one evening to announce that he was following his young brother's lead and joining the world of law enforcement.

Before Jed had chance to voice his first question – 'as a

bounty hunter?' – Shane produced his badge. In the short time he had been away from home. Shane Harding had joined the government. He was a deputy US marshal.

Shane was a changed man, he married local shop owner's daughter Millie and within a year he was a doting father of a baby boy.

'I wanted to call him Jed after my little brother,' Shane told him, 'but Millie thought you would prefer to be an uncle to a boy called Kyle, just like Pa.'

For a time the Hardings were like any other family until one fateful evening when the brothers just happened to be in the wrong place at the wrong time. They were walking down the deserted main street – the rest of the family, like most of the townsfolk, were in their homes – when two gunmen burst out of the town bank right in front of them.

Jed, as ever, was unarmed but before Shane could draw his gun from its holster, the bank robber's bullet ripped into his stomach. A second bullet caught Jed high on the shoulder and he was sent spinning backwards along the sidewalk. Shane managed to get off a single shot before a second bullet caught him full in the chest. Jed could only stare in horror as the two men rode out of town past the church and out into the night. Jed had managed only a glimpse of his brother's killer.

So at the age of 25 he abandoned his books to take up the law in another way – to join the US marshals office. Armed with his brother's guns and rifle and wearing the new badge of the marshal on his chest, he set out on his quest. What started out as a mission of revenge soon became a much greater cause. To uphold the law of the United States not only through the courts of justice but in the towns and cities where courthouses were the second choice for men who would rather shoot their way out of trouble than risk the threat of the noose. He stuffed his brother's marshal badge into his shirt pocket and became a man in search of a killer – a search that would give him no rest until he found his brother's killer.

When the face he had only glimpsed appeared on a wanted poster he began the search that eventually led him to the town of Alvorado.

Now, two years on, he was on the verge of running down his prey.

Lance McLagan had never envied his brother a thing. He was more than happy to let Roy and his cousin Brad be the ones who were his father's favourites, even though the old man often ridiculed them – especially Roy – in public and even in front of that nasty piece of work, the Mexican Juan Herrera.

Roy and Mex spent a lot of time together with Brad just tagging along, chasing girls and gambling.

The old man had put Roy in charge of the business in Alvorado but it was still his father's name that wielded the influence. And Roy knew that. Even Quince Leroy, the man who occupied the sheriff's office and wore the star as a token of his authority, paid little attention when Roy started giving the orders.

Lance always believed that his brother wanted so much more. Being the son of Alex McLagan was never going to be enough, and Lance knew that such ambition would land him in trouble again. The old man had covered up for many of Roy's brushes with the law. He tired of listening to the time that Roy beat the hell out of some poor kid up in San Juan County just because the boy objected to Roy moving in on his girl.

It was almost as though Roy had some kind of hold over his own father. . . .

So, no, Lance had no reason to envy his brother, except

. . . Amy Bannon.

He envied him Amy Bannon.

He hated the way that Roy treated his fiancée as though she was some casual dalliance like so many of his women.

Amy was about to become the next Mrs McLagan. Lance just wished that he was the lucky husband to be and not his brother.

Less than an hour ago he had left Roy cavorting with that drunken Mexican girl in the cantina but it was not the first time he had seen his brother being unfaithful to Amy. There had been many times when he had been tempted to tell her; to persuade her that she was choosing the wrong brother; that deep down Roy was no good. But he knew he never would. She would never believe him unless she saw it with her own eyes. The Roy she saw was the one he chose to show – courteous, considerate, ideal husband material.

But, worst of all, even if she learned the truth, Lance could never take his brother's place in Amy's affections. Even allowing for that, he was still in two minds about telling her what Roy was really like when they were not together.

However, as he rode away from the cantina, leaving his brother and some of the ranch hands to their drinking and fornicating pleasures, he knew he would never tell her the truth.

And it was not for Roy's sake. Or even for Amy's. It was his father.

For all his faults, Alex McLagan had been a good parent to his boys ever since their mothers died. Roy's decisions had been all his own.

On top of that, Alex and Jim Bannon, Amy's father, were friends and neighbours. For Amy to marry into the McLagan family would make both men happy. Jim

Bannon, instead of just being a neighbour on a small ranch that could have been swallowed up years ago during McLagan's empire-building days, would become a partner in the Big L. With Alex's health fading and Roy showing no interest other than taking the money it gave him, his old friend Jim would be the perfect addition to the family.

Lance was still thinking about all these things when he arrived at the huge, impressively decorated gate that led to the ranch house.

He was surprised to spot Amy returning from her afternoon picnic and she was not alone. He did not know the stranger riding alongside her buggy. He suspected that Roy might not like to hear about him.

Amy smiled at him when he rode up as she was stepping down from the buggy.

'Hello, Lance. I don't suppose you saw Roy anywhere while you were out riding?'

'Sorry, Amy, haven't seen him all day,' he lied, before turning to Matt and adding sharply: 'Who's this?'

'Lance. Meet Jack Duggan. We ran into each other down by the creek. He fixed the wheel on my buggy, the one that Roy's been promising to fix.'

Lance looked closely at the stranger, a tall, rangy man clearly used to hard work but with cold eyes. No sparkle. The face of a man who had spent a long time behind bars or on road work gangs, like so many of those who filled the saloons and whorehouses of Alvorado. Men on the run from the law in the north prepared to pay for protection.

'And what was he doing down by the creek?' Lance asked, turning towards Amy.

'Mr Duggan is looking for a job.'

Lance smiled. 'Well, you will have to tell him. . . .'

Matt suddenly stepped between them and they stood

facing each other. He was almost a head taller than the young McLagan.

'I'm right here, son and I speak the language, so you can talk to me. I don't need anybody to explain things. So what is it you want to tell me?'

Lance grinned. He was going to enjoy taking this stranger down a step, especially in front of Amy. Maybe she would be impressed.

'Well, mister, the thing is if you want to work around here you have to register.'

Matt gave him a puzzled look.

'I have to what?'

Lance glanced at Amy and smiled.

'Well, Mister Duggan who fixes buggy wheels, you haven't come this far without being told what you have to do.'

Matt shrugged.

'I met a couple of men on the trail who seemed to think they were important – some Mexican and a fat guy called Mitch. They didn't seem too bright to me, so maybe you ought to tell me.'

Matt was enjoying himself as Lance McLagan explained how all strangers arriving in Alvorado had to report to the town sheriff, who would put their name on a list and Alex McLagan would decide whether he wanted them out on the ranch.

He waited until Lance had finished his explanation with the warning: 'Oh, and I wouldn't go around saying insulting things about Mex and Mitch, else you may find Alvorado's not such a welcoming place.'

Matt remounted.

'Tell me something, young Lance. As Alex McLagan seems to own just about everything and everybody around these parts, what does he charge for the fresh air?'

He did not wait for an answer, touching his hat to Amy Bannon before turning his horse and, kicking it into a gallop, heading for the town.

CHAPTER SIX

Not for the first time, Quince Leroy was drinking alone. All around him the dice decks and card tables were crowded with half of the town's heavy gamblers while the rest stood by the long bar at the far end of the room.

Leroy toyed with his whiskey glass and stared at the girl in the emerald dress who was dealing cards at the blackjack table. But he was scarcely noticing her. He was a man alone in his own little world, a brooding haunted world from which he was beginning to believe there was no escape.

It had not always been like this, not when he first came to Alvorado when it was little more than a few shacks occupied by veterans from the Mexican wars. He, too, had been on the run from war, but a different war.

He had spent two war-torn years moving from town to town, job to job and it was now four years since he first entered New Mexico Territory still trying to wipe out the memory of his part in the '63 massacre in Lawrence, Kansas, when William Quantrill and his Raiders burned the stores, killed some 200 innocent civilians and became the most wanted men in the land.

At first, Leroy had been a minor figure, one of a small group of lookouts on Mount Oread as Quantrill mounted his attack on Lawrence shortly before 5 a.m. on August

21st. Once the guerilla leader had set up his headquarters at the Eldridge Hotel, the raiders split into smaller groups and Leroy then joined McLagan and his troops and played his part in the torching and killing. It was an action that turned Quince Leroy's life on its head. Four hours of looting and killing; the sight of a boy dying in his mother's arms – not from a stray bullet but from a shot fired deliberately through his young heart from the six-shooter of Alex McLagan, who followed this by hurling his torch into the back of the store. Then, as another child who must have been barely 12 years old raced to his mother's side, his own gun in his hand, firing as if of its own accord, aimed at the young boy's head. Leroy looked down in horror at the smoking gun in his grasp, turned and fled from the blazing building.

Separated from McLagan's group of looters, who had continued to ransack and burn the small street stores and homes, Leroy found himself in a deserted barn, where he hid until much of the shooting was over. He watched McLagan follow Quantrill and the rest ride out before saddling up a fresh horse and heading south.

Days later he had learned that Quantrill's Raiders had scattered far and wide, splintering into smaller gangs of bank and train robbers.

Leroy managed to steer clear of the war and when news of Quantrill's death at the hands of Union soldiers in Western Kentucky reached him and was followed soon afterwards by the surrender of Robert E Lee at Appomattox, the one-time Confederate sergeant felt he was home and free. He rarely gave his old commanding officer Alex McLagan another thought.

But the sight of the dying child, his own automatic action in shooting at the other boy, all so long ago, still haunted him.

He drank heavily, gambled and lost before eventually stumbling across the small settlement by accident, a beaten, broken man not caring whether he lived or died.

Fewer than fifty inhabitants – many of them survivors from the Mexican War of 1848 – occupied the few shacks, with a small general store that sold barely enough to keep body and soul together for Miguel the ageing owner and a one-room cantina. Back then it was The Town With No Name.

For some time Quince Leroy had lived the way he wanted – plenty of drink, a young Mexican girl to share his bed and cook his meals, a cantina owner who would keep his glasses filled for tales of the war in which gringos spent four years butchering each other.

The stories of his exploits with Jesse James and the Younger brothers may have been works of fiction but they guaranteed that his glass was never empty.

Then the day arrived when another of the renegades from Quantrill's men rode into town. Despite the increased girth and the thick red beard, Leroy had no problem in recognizing the man who was to rule his life. The war had been over for more than a year but it was coming back to claim him.

He had heard stories of the group of ranchers who had fought off gangs from the north and Mexico as well as renegade Apaches who had tried to move in on their territory. There had been heavy losses among the ranchers but one man had stood out as their leader and the rumours were that he had taken control of the western side of the valley some ten miles out of town.

It was the day that Leroy discovered that the man who had led those ranchers was his ex-army commander.

There were four of them, two younger men and a Mexican who could have been any age.

But it was the big man on the Pinto who had held Leroy's attention as he sat outside the cantina in the hot afternoon sun.

There was no mistaking Confederate Major Alex McLagan.

For a week, Leroy had stayed out of sight whenever McLagan and his men came into town but eventually his luck had to run out. He was leaning on the bar when it happened; a heavy hand landing squarely on his shoulder and he turned to find himself staring into the face of the man he believed would kill him if they ever met again.

But McLagan had not killed him; instead he had taken over his life. He had made him sheriff of a fast-growing town that was a refuge for men on the run, but the threat was always there.

Run out on me again, sergeant, and you are a dead man.

Now, as he sat alone with his whiskey bottle, Sheriff Quince Leroy was steeling himself to ignore the death threat. He was thinking of running out on Alex McLagan for the second time. Only this time it would be different – this time he would be leaving with a saddle-bag full of money, cash he had held back from the protection money he had collected on the old man's behalf. He would go tonight . . . or maybe tomorrow night.

McLagan thought he owned him – he thought everybody around the town of Alvorado had been bought and paid for. And maybe he was right but times were changing. Leroy was not going to stay around for the day when Roy McLagan and his gun-happy friends took over from the old man.

He drained his glass, refilled it with what was left in the bottle and returned to his desolate thoughts.

He hardly noticed when a fight broke out over one of the card tables and the pianist stopped playing. The two men, cowboys from the McLagan spread, exchanged blows but were too drunk to stand after only a couple of punches and staggered out of the saloon and on to the street.

Leroy finished his drink and stood up to leave. He would leave town soon. But maybe not tonight. Maybe tomorrow. . . .

There was a visitor waiting in his office when Leroy returned from the saloon but the last thing he needed was having to deal with another stranger looking for a safe place to escape the law.

Matt got up from his seat as Leroy entered the room.

'You left the door unlocked, Sheriff. I wouldn't have thought that was a good idea in a town like Alvorado.'

Leroy was in no mood for small talk. He grunted: 'Folk know better than to bring trouble down on this office, mister. What's your story?'

He slid into a chair behind the desk, reached inside one of the drawers and produced a folder containing a batch of wanted posters.

'Right, stranger. Which one of these is you?'

Matt leaned forward to check what the lawman was looking at.

'You won't find me in there, sheriff. I'm not on your list.'

Leroy looked the newcomer over. Tall, weather-beaten face, probably handsome in his younger days. He flipped through the pile of papers. The stranger was right. His picture wasn't there.

'So, what are you doing here in Alvorado if you ain't wanted by the law?'

Matt grinned.

'I didn't say that – I just said I'm not in there. At least, not yet.'

Leroy replaced the folder in the desk drawer.

'You expecting the law to come looking for you pretty soon, is that it?'

'Something like that,' Matt agreed. 'I'm looking for some place to set up for a spell before moving on. This place came highly recommended by some friends of mine up in Colorado. They spoke real well of it.'

Leroy was not interested in what friends in Colorado thought.

'You spoken to Alex McLagan yet?'

'Nope, but I did come across a couple of his cowhands and a pretty young woman on the way in here. The two at the entrance to the pass made it plain that I came to see you, sheriff. So here I am but, if that's wrong I'll gladly go see this man McLagan if he's the boss around here.'

'You'll find out if you stick around long enough. Now, what's your name?'

'Jack Duggan.'

Leroy scrawled the name on a sheet of paper.

'Then let's see your money, Mr Duggan. The two men at the entrance to the pass – they did explain it all to you, what you have to do?'

Matt made no move towards his pocket and the money he had taken from Kurt Brand's bedroom hideaway two days' earlier. He had already counted $700 but he had no intention of using more than a small part of that. He had promised old man Sam Dawson that he would return to the farm and it was a promise he intended to keep.

'I'd like you to tell me one thing, sheriff. What do I get for my money?'

Leroy rested his elbows on the desk and attempted to look Matt eye to eye.

'That kinda depends on what you are looking for and how much you've got to spend.'

'Let's say $200.'

Leroy paused before answering, keeping his eyes firmly on Matt's face.

Then, with a self-satisfied smirk, he said: 'That means you will probably earn your keep if Alex McLagan thinks you are worth the trouble of keeping around. Two hundred might buy you a job for a couple of weeks, maybe more.'

Matt made a pretence of giving the idea some thought.

'Let me make sure I've got this right, sheriff. I have to pay this man McLagan $200 and he will give me a job for two weeks. And for my $200 I get fed and a place in the bunkhouse. I pay him to work for him.'

Leroy was starting to enjoy himself.

'If you want his protection that's about it. Either pay up or leave town, Duggan. That's your choice.'

Matt knew he had pushed things as far as he could without giving the sheriff any reason to be suspicious so he peeled off $200 and tossed it towards the lawman.

'When do I get to meet my protector?'

Leroy slid the bills into the desk drawer.

'Go out to the ranch tomorrow morning. By then Alex will have been told about you by those men who stopped you, so be ready.'

'I'll be ready,' Matt said standing up. 'Now if you point me in the direction of the hotel I'll get myself a room for tonight before I move into the bunkhouse.'

'The McLagan Rooms are at the end of the street,' Leroy said, 'but let me give you some advice.'

'I'll gladly take it . . . if I like it.'

'Two things you should know, Duggan. I don't want to be scraping you off the main street any time soon. When you get to see Alex McLagan don't be fooled. His eyesight may be failing him but his brain isn't. What he can't see his son Roy will tell him. And if you think Alex is a mean critter then you'll really have something to worry about with Roy.'

Matt touched the brim of his hat in a mock salute.

'You said there were two things, Sheriff.'

'Yeah. That pretty young woman you met on the way in. That'd be Amy Bannon. Stay clear of her, Duggan. She's spoken for. She belongs to Roy McLagan and, like I said, Roy's the meanest of all the McLagans.'

'I'll bear that in mind, Sheriff. See you tomorrow.'

Jed Harding dismounted on the outskirts of the town. It had been a long ride and he was tired and hungry, just like his horse.

After watching the man who had called himself Jack Duggan go into the canyon, he had turned away and headed down a long-abandoned track that took him along a ridge towards Texas before turning again down a gradual slope and on to the plains. From there it was a straight ride around the McLagan spread, avoiding the fencing and night riders patrolling the boundary of the Big L.

Once beyond the ranch the way was open for a clear ride into town, especially under the cover of darkness. Jed Harding had never been a man to abandon caution – a bullet in the back could be just as deadly as one in the chest. And the killer he was hunting was not a man of scruples who believed in giving any man an even break. He had seen that with his own eyes and he still had the pain in his shoulder to remind him of that dark day.

Harding had reached the end of a long, lonely road. At times he had been close to despair but never had he been tempted to give up on the search.

Now, an acting lawman, sworn to uphold the laws of the United States and its territories, this was no longer a mission of revenge, but one in search of justice.

That's what Harding told himself as he settled down for the night in a disused barn on the edge of town.

Alex McLagan was getting used to sleepless nights. They had started almost a year ago, first with the headaches and then, more gradually, the eye strain. His sight was fading fast and although the headaches were bearable they still kept him awake most nights.

Like tonight.

He lay staring into the darkness but seeing nothing. His thoughts were far away.

McLagan had never shown any sign of weakness and he would not start now. To his two sons, his cowhands – the honest ones and the outlaws of Alvorado and other parts of eastern New Mexico – he was the boss. The Protector.

He had earned their respect and admiration. And their fear. But times were changing.

The war had been an annoying interruption to his plans to build a cattle empire. Sure, he reveled in the battles, then riding with Quantrill before breaking loose on his own, but McLagan was a cattleman and he had been among the first of the cowmen to head for the south for the vast open spaces of unused grazing lands of the New Mexico Territory.

Back then McLagan and men like him had to handle threats from Spaniards and Mexicans as well as hostile Indians. First it was the drives to army posts in the Territory and later to points on the railroads to Kansas at risk from massed attacks from Apache and Comanche. The principal shipping points were Dodge City, and Abilene and Newton in Kansas, and cattle were driven to these points from the ranges of west Texas and New Mexico.

It was so much easier now for the likes of Roy and Lance and the others from across the plains towards El Paso. The railroads were changing everything. No more month-long cattle drives, shooting up small towns or losing more than a hundred head.

Soon it would all be Roy's and he was not cut out to be a cattleman. Trouble was his middle name and Alex's only crumb of comfort was that he would not be around to see his eldest son gunned down in some stinking saloon or whorehouse. Amy Bannon would then be a young widow – that was if the pair ever got around to marrying.

Alex was a worried man. He knew that Roy would not rest until he controlled half of New Mexico, and then even that would not be enough. There would always be somebody who would be waiting for him . . . down a darkened alleyway, out on the range, even in a crowded saloon.

The rapid approach of old age had opened the eyes of the man who had once ruled by terror, by the power of the bullet. He had killed because they were times for killing. But he was in his sixty-eighth year and he realized he had little time left.

He wished Lance could have been a bit more like him but his younger son was his mother's boy, quiet, reliable and even tempered. He didn't even wear a sidearm.

That left only the Mexican. Sure, he had been useful in the old days when quarrels had to be settled with a gun. Mex was quick and accurate but, like Roy, eventually he would end up eating dirt and be instantly forgotten.

Those days were closer than Alex McLagan could possibly imagine when he eventually dozed off shortly before dawn.

The days of the McLagan Empire and the town built in Hell were numbered.

Matt Brogan stirred in his hotel room, wakened by the noise from across the street. The sound of breaking glass and gunfire. It was an hour after midnight.

There were screams and shouts, and when he made his way to the window he saw the reason. Outside the Diamond Bar, six men were involved in a brawl, rolling in the dust, fists and boots flying as two of the saloon's show-girls shouted encouragement from the doorway.

A couple of old-timers were firing shots aimlessly into the night sky and dancing a drunken jig around the fighting cowboys. Matt stood at the window, watching for several minutes before deciding that Alvorado was no place for decency or law-abiding citizens. The town's reputation as a hideaway for the men who scorned law and order was well earned. Quince Leroy was nothing more than a tax collector; the town was McLagan's town and although Matt had ridden in with his eyes wide open and one plan in mind – kill or be killed – he realized that he might need to change that plan.

From what he had gathered from his visit to the sheriff's office, McLagan was tied to the ranch and Roy, the wayward son, went his own way.

Alex's eyesight was failing so the test would come when he came face to face with Roy, who Leroy had called the worst of them all.

But Matt no longer wanted to see Roy McLagan dead. That would be no revenge. Everybody dies sooner or later. Roy would not get off so easily for what he did to the Brogan family. He would be destroyed first.

The old man's oncoming blindness was enough punishment and, as for the Mexican, Matt would have no regrets if he had to put a bullet in his head but he wanted him to know it was coming and he wanted him to know why.

He watched the street brawl fizzle out and then decided there was time to get some more sleep before he rode out to the Big L and meet Alex McLagan.

*

The sun was rising when Jed Harding left the abandoned barn and made his way into town.

The main street was quiet – empty except for a stray dog dozing in the shade offered by a horse trough and an ageing storekeeper who was sweeping the boardwalk.

He looked up but turned away almost at once. Strangers were common in Alvorado. None of them stayed around long enough to become neighbours. This man, who sat tall in the saddle and had the look of somebody who knew his business, would be no exception. He was just another stranger on the run.

Life would go on for the storekeeper for as long as he was prepared to pay Alex McLagan his protection money.

Jed rode slowly past the saloon and the sheriff's office, and dismounted outside the hotel at the end of the street.

A barber's shop stood on the corner and he needed a shave and haircut – and definitely a bath – before he did anything else including finding an eating place for his breakfast.

He had waited a long time for this day – since he started the search for the man who had killed his brother and put a bullet in his shoulder. He was also the man who had caused Jed's mother to die of a broken heart.

That killer was somewhere in Alvorado and whether he left the town dead or alive was up to him.

The barber appeared in his doorway and threw down a part-smoked cheroot before turning and going back inside. Jed followed him into the shop.

The barber was short, round-faced and overweight. He walked with a slight limp.

'Take a seat, mister. Shave or haircut?'

'Both,' Jed said, taking the nearest seat and preparing

for a long, one-way discussion. But it never came. The barber shaved him and cut his hair in silence, until he suddenly said: 'New in town?'

'Just passing through,' Jed told him, and the man chuckled.

'Sure, mister. Tell me to keep my nose out of it. That'll be 50 cents.'

Jed gave him the money.

'What are you trying to tell me?'

'Nobody passes through Alvorado. Leastways not without the permission of Alex McLagan, and I know you haven't been here long enough to get that. You pay to stay here and you pay to leave. Only two kinds of men come here – men on the run or men looking for somebody on the run.'

'And you want to know which one I am?'

The barber shook his head. 'Nope. I don't want to know anything about you, that way I can't tell no lies when they come calling after somebody reports seeing a new stranger in town who called into Dan Becker's barber's shop.'

Jed examined his shave and haircut in a large mirror. He felt cleaner.

'Tell me, Mr Becker, why do you stay here if it's so bad?'

'Where would I go? I've lived here since before McLagan and his crew moved in. I cut hair and give shaves and I don't cause trouble. Anyways, even the drifters who come here need a shave or a haircut occasionally. My wife's long gone so I reckon I'll still be here when the time comes to put me in a box.

'But I will say this, stranger, if McLagan doesn't know you're here now he soon will so I'd move on right now if I was you.'

Jed replaced his hat, brushed loose hair off his shoulders and smiled: 'Thanks for the advice. I'll think about it but I reckon I'd like to meet this Mr McLagan.'

He left the barber shop, stood on the sidewalk and breathed in the morning air.

It was then that he noticed him, leaving the hotel on the far corner of the street.

He had promised to buy him a drink in return for a cup of coffee. He said his name was Jack Duggan. That was only a little lie. Harding knew exactly who the man across the street was and why he was in town.

Matt Brogan left his hotel and stepped out into the sunlight. The street was deserted except for a man striding out of the barber's shop on the opposite corner.

He was looking in Matt's direction but made no move to cross the street – just two strangers going their separate ways.

The ride out to the McLagan spread gave Matt time to go over his plans. Coming face to face with the man who had murdered his wife and son and burned his house had dominated his thoughts for three long years, with vengeance high on his list.

It should have been enough time to abandon the hate that would have led him into a straight shootout with all three of the killers. Some of that hate had been replaced by a cold, calculated decision that the lives of the McLagans were too small a price to pay for what they had done to his family.

He would gamble all on passing through the scrutiny of the father and son, just as he had when he faced the Mexican at the pass. He would work his way into their confidence and then . . . slowly he would destroy them and all they stood for.

Matt Brogan did not like himself for what he was planning but prison had hardened him and now his freedom, earned at a heavy cost in his breakout, had made him all the more determined to carry out the job.

The entrance to the McLagan ranch was as he expected – a wide gate, above which was a pair of longhorns, a Big L sign and underneath that the words: You Are On McLagan Land.

Matt mockingly doffed his hat and rode through. He rode on towards his date with destiny. In less than an hour he would come face to face with the killer of his family.

Alex McLagan leaned heavily on the rail around the verandah and stared out at the snowcapped high peaks in the Sangre de Cristo mountain range.

McLagan liked to know that all he could see from his favourite spot was part of the Big L, but that was growing smaller each day as his eyesight faded. He could no longer pick out the peaks in the distance and even the much closer ponderosa pine trees were little more than a blur.

And McLagan had discovered that it was not only his eyes that were failing. Two visits to specialist doctors in Santa Fe had confirmed what he had guessed ever since the headaches and stomach pains started. He was on borrowed time. Six months, maybe a year – that was how long he had according to the doctors. That had been eight months ago, so time was running out fast.

Yet there was still so much to do. Age may have mellowed the old man but he could not say the same for his elder son. Roy was no good. He would never make a rancher; he would never work. Alex had known that since Roy was just a kid when he would pick a fight with anybody who crossed him. By the time he was in his early teens, fists had turned to knives – then guns – until, at the age of 18 years, he had killed a man in a drunken brawl.

The victim was a drifter, a hobo without friends who had

been in the wrong place at the wrong time – the Silver Bullet Saloon in the backwater town of Resolution.

Witnesses had confirmed that Roy shot the stranger in self-defence – though their evidence came only after a little persuasion.

As the years passed he had become even wilder, freer with his gun, and what happened when Roy was away from the ranch his father could only guess.

Alex had forgotten how many times he had called Roy in for father-to-son chats; how many times the boy had promised to change, to become worthy of taking over the Big L when the time came.

'Roy, my boy, I'm a cattleman – always have been. You know I'm hoping you'll feel the same, you'll want to build something you can be proud of . . . something to give to your family when you have kids of your own. Promise me, son, promise me you'll settle down.'

It was the first time that Alex McLagan had ever pleaded for anything in his life. But he instantly knew that it was pointless.

'But you've got years in you yet, Pa,' Roy had told him, before going out to carry on where he had left off, drinking and whoring.

Only young Lance kept Alex away from total despair. But did he have the will or the strength to do the job? Once he had hoped that Lance could have been more like his brother. But no longer.

The old man winced again as the stabbing pain attacked his stomach. He had not slept well and had risen before dawn.

Roy had not been home all night but that was no surprise. Alex had hoped the reason for that was he had stayed over at the Bannon place but he knew that was not the case. Amy's father, Jim, may have been old man

McLagan's friend but he had never approved of Roy and the proposed marriage to Amy, so any chance his son had of staying overnight at the Bannons was unthinkable.

Alex wiped the sweat away from his face and turned to go back into the house. It was time to make a decision. Sometime today he would get the brothers together, along with their cousin Brad, and tell them the truth. He was handing over – not to Roy or Lance – but to his friend and neighbour Jim Bannon. And if Amy did not want to tie herself to somebody like Roy, that would be her choice.

As he turned to go inside he saw a rider approaching. Probably one of his son's drinking friends. Well, he had come to the wrong place if he was looking for Roy.

Alex slumped into the nearest chair and closed his eyes. The pain was still there. Perhaps the doctors had been optimistic about the length of time he had left.

He reached for an unfinished glass of whiskey left over from the previous night. It didn't help.

Matt Brogan slowed his horse to a walk as he approached the large two-storey ranch house that was centre point of the Big L. He could just make out the figure leaning on the rail of the verandah. The man seemed to be gazing out at the distant mountain range, surveying his kingdom. Matt took him to be Alex McLagan, owner of the Big L and The Protector who controlled everything and everybody in the valley around Alvorado. The man stretched, leaned forward and then turned and went into the house.

Matt knew that his moment had come. The man he had escaped from prison to track down and to make pay for destroying his family was within reach. But he felt no sense of triumph, no pending satisfaction that his wife and son were about to be avenged. Katie and Toby were dead; the death of Alex McLagan would not bring them back. Even when he finally put a bullet into one of the men responsible they would still be dead.

He pulled his horse to a halt and leaned forward in his saddle. Eventually, he nudged his horse into motion and five minutes later he was mounting the steps into the ranch house.

Alex McLagan was slumped in an armchair on the far side of a large heavily furnished room; his legs spread-eagled out in front of him, his arms hanging limply over the sides of the chair. His head hung limply to one side, his eyes closed. On the carpet down to his right was an empty whiskey glass, the contents having spilled out on to the floor.

Matt edged his way into the room.

'McLagan?' he tried but got no response, no sign that he had been heard. He tried again. Still no reply. He moved forward and leaned over the figure – a man in his late sixties, Matt guessed. His eyes were closed and his pale features were twisted as though he could still feel pain even in sleep. He groaned feebly at Matt's gentle touch.

If this was the Alex McLagan that he had spent three years vowing to kill he would have to act soon. The old man, a pale shadow of the witness who had stood in front of a judge and sworn that he had seen Matt kill his own family, was already close to death.

CHAPTER SEVEN

Matt stood up and turned to leave but never quite made it to the door. As he spun around he found himself staring up at the top of the staircase and into the barrel of a gun. It was in the hands of the young man he had met the previous day, Lance McLagan.

'Hold it right there, mister.' Lance started down the stairs. 'Back off,' he said, waving the gun. Then: 'Pa! You awake, Pa?'

Matt did as he was ordered and stepped away.

'I'm not the one you should be worrying about, son. Seems to me that the old man is in need of a doctor – and fast.'

Lance hurried down the stairs, his gun still firmly gripped in his left hand, and pointed at Matt's chest. But as he reached the foot of the staircase he lost all interest in his visitor.

He leaned over the man in the chair. 'Pa? Wake up.'

Alex McLagan's only response was another feeble groan.

Matt moved in. 'Like I said, son, he's in a bad way, and if it isn't from too much whiskey then I reckon you have got a big problem.'

Lance turned to face him. There was a look of panic in

his young face. His father was not supposed to be ill. He was never ill, not in all the years Lance had been old enough to know.

'What do I do, mister? What – what happened?'

Matt studied the kid's face. He couldn't just walk away and leave the old man to die. He knew he had to help.

'Is there anybody else in the house?' he asked.

Lance shook his head. Roy had not come home all night. He had no idea where his brother was and right now he didn't care.

'Then it's up to you. I suggest you get out there, hitch up that buckboard I saw on my way in here and get your father in to town to see a doctor.'

Lance nodded. 'There's no doctor in Alvorado. At least not one who'll be sober. The nearest town is more than two hours' ride.'

'Then I reckon we should get moving,' Matt snapped.

Lance didn't argue. He raced out on to the verandah, leaving Matt alone with the man he had spent so long planning to bring to justice, either by bullet or noose. Now he was trying to save his life.

He lifted McLagan out of his seat and carried him from the house. He weighed next to nothing, a skeletal shadow of the man whose evidence had condemned him to a fifteen-year sentence in a penitentiary.

Alex McLagan deserved to die – but not like this. Matt needed him alive, at least until he discovered what really happened the night his own life was destroyed.

CHAPTER EIGHT

Jed Harding had dealt with evil men many times. Killers, rapists, train and bank robbers had all combined to persuade him to believe that there was no good left in the world.

But he knew that to be a falsehood. Good men still held sway and even in a town like Alvorado there would be men and women who believed in a society of law and order.

His job now was to find them. He was way out of his territory. His badge, now hidden away in his saddle-bag, would not have helped him. He would have to rely on the persuasion of a gun.

But he was not going to let that stop him from carrying out the job he had set himself. He would need the help of honest men. The killer of his brother could be walking among them.

But where to find those honest folk?

He could think of only one place to start his search but as he approached the small neglected chapel on the outskirts of town he held out little hope of finding the kind of person he needed to help him. He pushed open the creaking gate that was already hanging loose and strolled up the short weed-strewn path, more in blind faith than expectation.

The chapel was just as he had expected to find it – deserted. The dust-covered pews and broken, overturned chairs were all the evidence he needed to tell him that the good folk of Alvorado were too few to require the use of a church.

Harding had never been a religious man. He had come face to face with too many killers and thieves to find enough time to think about a benevolent God but, despite his own lack of faith, he felt a huge sadness that a place of worship had been reduced to a shattered shell. He allowed himself a smile when he realized that, on entering the building, he had, as a token of respect, removed his hat.

Up to his left, the sun shone in through a broken window and through the gap left by a few missing wooden wall panels.

After a lengthy look around the abandoned room, he turned to leave but as he reached the door he came face to face with a tall, thin man dressed in the black he associated with the cloth of the clergy. Harding guessed he was in his late fifties. He was carrying a garden spade and had the sweat-soaked appearance of a man who had been hard at work in the morning sun.

'Good morning, mister,' he said, his voice high-pitched, but it gave Harding the feeling that there was something of the genuine welcome in it. 'What brings you here? Can't say I've seen you in town before so you're not from the Big L. Can I help you?'

Harding walked out to meet him. 'I guess maybe you can if you happen to be the preacher here.'

The man smiled but, unlike the welcome, it was forced. 'I was – a long time ago. Alvorado has no time for religion now.'

Harding jerked his thumb over his shoulder. 'I've seen inside.'

'There was a time when those pews were filled with God-fearing people, young and old, men and women.'

The man fell silent as though memories of those old days still caused him pain.

Then he said: 'My name is Jonathon Elwell.'

He stretched out his hand and Harding shook it. For a man who, on closer scrutiny, looked frail and older than he had first appeared, his grip was firm and strong.

'Jed Harding.'

'And I was right – you are new in town.'

He moved forward, nudged Harding gently aside and said: 'Come in. I have a small house out back. I'm sure I can offer you a coffee and you can tell me what brings you to Alvorado, unless, of course, it is what brings most people here and you don't look the kind.'

'And what kind is that, Mr Elwell?' he asked, although he already knew the answer.

'The sort who needs the protection of Alex McLagan,' the man said, smiling again, only this time there was genuine warmth. 'Gunfighters, bank and train robbers, escaped convicts – we get a good mix here.'

It was the opening Harding had hoped for.

'There must be some decent folk, law-abiding citizens even in a town like this.'

'Oh, yes, there are some spread around the district but most are clever enough not to come into town very often. They keep to their own little farms and let the town and its citizens continue their journey to Hell.'

Harding followed the retired clergyman down the aisle of the abandoned church and into a garden at the back. They walked along a path through a small thicket and emerged in front of a single-storey building, a whitewashed brick and wooden structure that, unlike the chapel, had benefited from some loving care. As they neared the door of the house, Harding spotted a small plot surrounded by a low white picket fence. At the far end, in the shade of a young tree, was a headstone.

Elwell saw his visitor pause and look.

'My wife, Martha,' he said, pausing at Harding's shoulder.

Harding studied the headstone. Martha Elwell. Born 1829 – Died August 1 1868. Thirty-nine years old.

Harding asked. 'How did she die?'

Elwell did not answer at once and Harding could see that the memory of his wife's death still caused him heartache.

'Sadly, she was just another innocent victim of the violence that has plagued this town for too long.' Without elaborating, he turned away from the burial plot and headed for the house. Then he added suddenly: 'It's that grave that keeps me here, Mr Harding. It may sound un-Christian and one day I will have to seek God's forgiveness but I will not leave until the day I see the man responsible for my wife's death take his own place under the soil.'

Jed followed the man into the house. Inside was the kind of room that reminded him of his childhood – compact, comfortably furnished with a pair of armchairs near an open hearth, a large table dominating the room and shelves decorated with pottery. In the far corner there was a desk but, instead of containing the usual writing or reading implements of notepaper and pens, it had been turned into a personal shrine. Unlit candles in silver holders stood either side of a large, framed picture of a pretty woman in her thirties. Jed guessed it to be the late Martha Elwell. The only book on the desk was a large Bible.

Elwell saw his visitor examining the desk and its contents.

'I may have ceased preaching, Mr Harding but that is a comfort to me, you understand.'

Elwell left the room via a door next to the desk and returned minutes later carrying two mugs of coffee.

'I could offer you something stronger if you wish,' Elwell said, 'but you don't look like the sort of man who takes liquor before noon. Am I right?'

Jed grinned. 'Almost,' he said, taking the coffee mug. Despite his experience as a lawman, and well aware of the dangers of first impressions, he had taken an instant liking to the retired preacher. They each slid a chair away from the table and sat facing each other.

'Now, Mr Harding, how can I help?'

Jed curled his fingers around the coffee mug. There would be no better time or place to take somebody on trust. If Jonathon Elwell was not what he appeared to be – an honest clergyman still grieving for a wife who had been dead for two years – then his chances of finding the man he was hunting would be lost. He decided it was worth the chance.

'Like you, sir, I have lost somebody to a gunman and there's a connection with the town of Alvorado.'

He expected a reaction but the man opposite waited for him to continue.

'I have been trailing the man who killed my brother.

'Shane was a US marshal living with his wife and child in a small, out of the way town in eastern Arizona where nothing much ever happened. The occasional saloon brawl was the worst it got for the people of Oakville and Shane could handle that without any call for gunplay.

'I was walking the street with him one night – I guess we should have been at home with the rest of the family. It was all quiet checking the doors of local businesses and stores when he spotted a lamp on in the bank. Shane knew the owner often worked late so at first he thought little of it. He was a friend of James Kane who owned the Oakville Bank and he often called in for a late-night chat and a glass or two of the whiskey the old man kept locked away in his desk drawer. But on this particular night he remembered that it was Kane's daughter's birthday and the notion that her father would be working late into the night did not seem likely, so after checking the hardware store and the livery stable he decided to investigate.

'But just as we crossed the alley between his own office and the bank, a rider came out of the darkness and knocked him to the ground. As he scrambled to get back on to his feet there was a gunshot from inside the bank. A man came rushing out and leapt on to the spare horse the other rider had been leading.

'Before he could draw his gun, my brother was hit in the chest by two bullets. A third caught me high on the shoulder. I was unarmed and the bank robbers raced off into the night.

'Shane died an hour later on the doctor's table. James Kane was already dead in his own bank.

'I got a quick glance at one of the killers and I swore then that I would hunt them down. It's been two years and I've been following every lead ever since.'

'And those leads finally brought you to Alvorado?' Elwell interrupted. 'Are you a lawman?'

'I was studying law with the idea of becoming an attorney,' Jed told him. 'But when Shane died I decided that I could do better if I followed him so I became a US marshal.

'Oakville had a young sheriff, an inexperienced kid called Ben Dexter, who tried his best but there was not much he could do with a posse of six willing men who tracked them as far as they could, but they were deep into Indian Territory when they had to give up. Young Ben gave me all the information he had, including a description he picked up, and left me to it.

'The bank's new owners put up a $2,000 reward for information leading to the arrest of the killers but even bounty hunters gave it up as a lost cause.

'I had been tracking them for months without much luck but one name kept cropping up. It was not a man's name and it was spoken quietly by the sort of men on the run from the law, or escaped prisoners.'

'Let me guess,' said the clergyman draining the last of his coffee. 'The name was Alvorado.'

'And that's why I am here, Reverend. This town is a known hideaway and the perfect place for the men who killed my brother and the bank manager. And I need your help.'

Jonathon Elwell got to his feet and moved off to refill the coffee mugs.

'And you have it, Mr Harding, and it's gladly given.'

Matt Brogan pulled the wagon up alongside the doctor's rooms that doubled as a hospital halfway along the main street of the small town of Santa Rosa. He had learned little during the two-hour ride from the Big L. Lance McLagan was far more interested in the health of his sick father than talking to this stranger, who had been so helpful but could still be responsible for his father's present state. He knew that was unreasonable but he had to blame somebody – for something.

Roy was nowhere to be found and that useless Mexican Herrera was probably with him, either drunk or still bedding one of the girls in the cantina.

God, how he hated his life on the Big L. Even as a young kid when his mother was alive and he saw so little of his father he would rather have spent time with his books than working on the ranch, chopping wood or fixing fences. Or even rounding up filthy stray steers.

But Roy, well he was different. He had once idolized the old man and hung on every word of the stories of their father's exploits in the Mexican War of 1846. He was there from the start – at the Battles of Palo Alto and Resaca de la Palma – and Roy insisted on hearing every tale from the border conflicts.

Alex was only happy to oblige. The Mexicans had already been demoralized by disastrous wars with the Comanche and Apaches and had little fight left in them. The skirmishes were brief but brutal and Roy McLagan wanted to hear about every last drop of blood that was shed on the battlegrounds.

But he resented that he had been left behind while his father was off fighting in the Civil War and he was less than happy when the old man relayed all the gory details of battles up north. Roy was never given to smiling.

And then there was Amy Bannon. What did she see in Roy and his swaggering friends? Lance thought about Amy a lot. If only Roy would keep one of his promises and show her some respect, perhaps he could live with that.

'You gonna help me get him inside, kid?'

The question broke into his thoughts and together they carried the old man into the small wooden construction that was the town's hospital. They were met by a doctor and a middle-aged nurse, who directed them through to a room at the back of the building.

By now the old man had regained consciousness and was breathing a lot easier, though he was still sweating heavily.

The doctor ordered them to lie him on the only empty bed in the room and leaned over to examine him. Matt stood back while the doctor gave his nurse some instructions. She hurried away and between them Lance and the doctor did their best to make the old man comfortable.

As he moved away towards the door, Matt saw Alex McLagan raise his head from the pillow and stretch out an arm in his direction. Whether it was a gesture of thanks or pointing a finger of recognition, Brogan could not decide.

He went outside and smoked a cheroot before unhitching his horse from the back of the wagon and checking his saddle straps.

Stubbing out the remains of his smoke underfoot, he turned to see young Lance standing in the open doorway.

'Just like to say thanks, mister. I reckon that without you the old man may have died on me before I could get help.'

'Glad to be useful, son,' Matt replied. 'You ought to stay around here for the rest of the day.'

Lance nodded. 'Reckon so, though I got to let Roy know that Pa's out here in a bad way. He says thanks, by the way, for your help.'

'He is in a fit state to talk, then?' Matt tried to keep the surprise out of his voice.

Lance gave a half smile.

'It takes more than a heart attack to keep Alex McLagan quiet.'

Matt climbed into the saddle.

'Did he say anything else?'

Lance did not answer at once but appeared to be thinking about his reply.

'Only to say that, well, he owes you big time, Mr Duggan.'

'Tell him I'll drop by sometime and he can thank me in person,' Matt said. He touched his hat and turned away.

You never said a truer word in your entire life, Alex McLagan, he thought as he rode off towards Alvorado.

Lying in the hospital bed, Alex McLagan stared up at the ceiling. His mind was in a spin. Who was that stranger? And where had he seen his face before?

CHAPTER NINE

Brogan unsaddled his horse, paid the livery stable man his dollar for the animal's keep and strolled back to his hotel.

The long ride back from the hospital to Alvorado had taken him around the Big L ranch, and although there was little activity it gave him an idea of the size of the spread the McLagans owned. Nearby, there was a row of horses tethered to a rail.

Matt studied the scene. Alex McLagan was in a hospital two hours ride to the south; his young son Lance was at his bedside, so the only McLagan who could be at home was Roy.

The line of horses showed that he was not alone in the house, so Matt decided there would be better times to confront the man who had condemned him to three years of hell. He turned his horse and headed for town.

The sun was fading in the west by the time he bedded his horse down in the stable, and as he made his way along the street towards his hotel his attention was drawn to the noise coming from The Diamond Bar.

It had been more than three years between drinks and a man can work up a hell of a thirst in three years, so he pushed open the batwings and edged into the saloon.

Nobody took any notice of the stranger. They were

either deep in their card games or busy fondling the dancing girls giggling in mock protest as they tried to dance on the low stage at the far end of the bar. He made his way to a vacant table in the corner of the room.

Matt ordered his beer and settled into the empty chair with his back to the wall.

He studied the faces in the room and allowed his mind to wander back to the days when he too would have been a saloon bar regular, playing cards deep into the night before picking up the prettiest girl he could find – and there were not many who were pretty, he recalled – before spending the night in some dingy bedroom.

He convinced himself that he had his reasons and they were not his fault. His mother had died when he was only 9 years old and his father, a failed stage company owner, had left him to fend for himself at the age of 16. Will Brogan had fled to Tennessee with the woman who had been in charge of his office. Her husband never suspected.

Matt found himself drawn into the company of shiftless young cowboys who were more interested in drink than work.

Then, by chance, he and the others rolled out of a saloon a lot worse for drink one afternoon and he had literally bumped into Katie Miller. One of the group – he couldn't remember any of the names – had made some lewd suggestion and tried to follow it up by grabbing the young lady around the waist and pulling her into him.

Matt stepped in, dragged him off and sent him spinning into the dust.

'I'm sorry about that, miss, my friend didn't mean any harm – it's just that we've been celebrating and. . . .' He felt himself struggling for words after that. This young woman was such a beauty as he had ever seen before and when she smiled at him he knew that his life was about to change.

It was the last he saw of his aimless cowboys and saddle tramps who had become his friends and the start of the rest of his life.

He became a young deputy in the town of Broken Hill, married his girl and Toby was born. Then came the move to Colorado and the small ranch. Life was perfect . . . until that fateful return from Denver.

Now all that was gone. He was here in this town that God had abandoned and he was looking for vengeance.

'Can I fill your glass?'

He looked up to see a tall, broad figure standing opposite. The man was smiling down at him.

'You are Jack Duggan?'

'That's me. But do I know you?'

'I did promise to buy you a drink if I saw you again. We met on the trail the other night. I shared your coffee.'

The pair shook hands.

'I remember,' Matt said at last. 'Jed, isn't it?'

'Jed Harding. Another beer?'

Without waiting for an answer, Harding walked over to the bar, returned with two glasses of beer and pulled up a chair.

Matt took the glass and eyed the man. He remembered that Harding had told him that he had business in New Mexico but he had never said where. Was it a coincidence that they had met up again in Alvorado?

'What brings you to this hellhole of a town?'

'I could be asking you the same question, Jack.'

'True,' Matt nodded, 'but as I reckon it's none of your business I don't have to answer. But thanks for the beer anyway.'

'Like I said, I owed you,' Harding replied, 'but I can see I was wrong about you. I'll wish you goodnight.' He got up to leave but something made Matt speak out.

'Look, Jed, I'm sorry. It's been a bad day. You don't have to go.'

Harding retook his seat. The two men shook hands for a second time.

'I watched you from a ridge yesterday when you passed through the canyon leading here. The two guards didn't seem too pleased to see you, so I guessed this was your first time. And since I hadn't seen your face on any posters I hoped you were on the side of the good guys.'

'And you?' Matt interrupted. 'Are you on the side of the angels?'

Jed toyed with his glass before answering. He had trusted the preacher, now it was time to trust another.

'Can I trust you, Jack? If that is the name you are using.'

'It's as good as any for now. Try me. But let me guess first. You're a lawman and you are here to catch somebody. A killer probably because you are way out of your territory.'

There was an awkward silence before Harding said: 'Which are you, Jack? Are you running from the law – or are you here to settle a score?'

'My reasons for being here aren't your problem. Let's just say that I'm not the man you are looking for.'

'I believe you. One of the reasons I'm in town is to find the man who killed my brother. He was just 27 years old, an honest lawman in the quiet town of Oakville, Arizona, when he was gunned down while doing his rounds. I was there. I saw it happen. He was the father of a young child and husband of a pretty wife.

'It was only when I was going through his personal effects that I discovered a letter notifying him that he had been accepted as a federal agent, part of a special squad set up on the orders of the President.

'Grant had preached about how it was a long journey back to the status of a full Union of the States. The war may have been over but Shane decided to join the special service that was formed to track down dissidents in the south who were hell bent on keeping the hatred alive.

'It's true that most of that is now just bitterness and grudging acceptance that we are all one nation but there are still men who think they are beyond the law. I became another of those government agents and one of my jobs is to chase them down. It became personal when Shane was killed, so you could say I'm on private business.'

Matt said nothing. There was more to come from the man sitting across the table.

'It's the government's belief that this town is a hotbed for rebels just waiting for the right time to renew hostilities.'

Matt tried to hide a grin but failed.

'And they sent you here single-handed to find a man who killed your brother but had no connection with any dissidents and while you are here snuff out any flickering spark of a return to Civil War? Good luck, Mr Harding – I reckon you're going to need it.'

He stood up and made to leave the saloon.

'What I need is some help.'

'And you're looking at me to offer it?' Matt reached inside his pocket, threw a coin on to the table. 'I'll buy you a beer but that's the best I can do. I've got my own business to attend to and then I'm on my way.'

Harding picked up the dollar, twirled it between finger and thumb and then looked straight up at Matt.

'Sorry to hear that. It looks as though I've got you all wrong after all.'

Puzzled by Harding's tone, Matt stood motionless and waited for the lawman to go on.

'I said I believed you when you told me you aren't the man I'm looking for and that's true. But that doesn't mean

I believe everything else you've told me.'

He reached inside his shirt and pulled out a sheet of paper, which he carefully unfolded and placed on the table.

'Your real name is Matt Brogan and you were serving a fifteen-year prison sentence until a few days ago for killing your wife and son.'

Matt was stunned. So Harding knew who he was . . . that he was on the run like almost everybody else in Alvorado. And yet . . . he was still asking him for help.

He returned to his chair.

'How long have you known?'

'Since I watched you escape from that road gang. I already knew you would be heading this way.'

Matt made to interrupt but Harding hurried on: 'You asked a lot of questions while you were in the pen, and most of the answers came out as Alvorado. So I figured that the men who put you inside must be out this way and you would come looking for them.'

Matt thought for a moment before putting the question.

'You know who I am, what I am – but still you are looking to me to help you. Why?'

Harding refolded the sheet of paper and returned it to his breast pocket.

'Yours was a famous case. When you made your prison break, you couldn't have done it without help so all we had to do was ask a few questions; not every convict is an honourable member of the human race, so we offered a little incentive and I was on your trail within hours.'

When he saw the puzzled frown on Matt's face he went on.

'I looked into the details of your case and as soon as I learned who the witnesses were and where they were supposedly "upright citizens" I figured that you may have been telling the truth.'

'Well, thanks for that, anyway.'

Harding finished his beer.

'It wasn't just a hunch. When I learned who was the circuit judge who heard the evidence and convinced the jury to convict you I was sure you were innocent.'

'The judge?'

'Henry Coburn from Santa Fe. That's just thirty or so miles out of Alvorado, mighty close to the Big L ranch of the McLagans. If you've got a devious mind like mine then, boy, that is suspicious, especially for two things.'

'Tell me.'

'There have been stories about how Coburn's judgements are likely to be favourable to anybody who has the right amount of money, and evidence can be overlooked for the right price.'

'And you think the McLagans paid him to make sure I went to prison for something they did?'

'Maybe . . . maybe not,' Harding muttered. 'Could be they didn't have to pay him.'

Matt waited for an explanation and when it came it answered everything.

'Henry Coburn's wife of thirty years is the sister of Alex McLagan. Coburn is the old man's brother-in-law.'

Abe Jackson turned away from the bar and went back to his table. Sheriff Quince Leroy, Deke Harris, owner of Alvorado's gunsmiths, and Pete Sherwood, the town's blacksmith, were already losing patience with the mayor. Three times he had left the table to talk to the bartender and each time he had returned with a face that looked a lot more sour than when he had left.

'What's getting into you, Abe? Ain't we supposed to be in a card game?'

It was Harris who challenged Jackson but the mayor just shook his head and retrieved his cards from the table.

'Then I suggest we get on with it and quit the chatter.'

Jackson studied his cards – they amounted to nothing worth holding and he grunted his disgust, throwing them on to the table. His impatience grew as he watched the others play, the hand ending with Leroy sweeping up the money.

But as he prepared to deal again, Jackson gripped his arm.

'Hold it, Sheriff. We've got to talk.'

Leroy grinned.

'Talk? What's to talk about when I'm on a winning streak? It can wait.'

Abe Jackson reddened. He wasn't accustomed to being spoken to like that by the hired help. And that was all Quince Leroy was – hired help. Or, in his case, a hired gun, just the same as everybody who worked for the McLagans.

'We got to talk. And I mean now.'

Deke Harris was not the sort to miss out on a chance to ride the bogus lawman.

'Guess you ought to run along, Quince, just in case Alex finds out you've been wasting time in the saloon when you should be out there hunting the bad guys. Ain't the town full of them?'

Leroy scowled but moved away from the table and followed Jackson to another table.

Jackson signaled to the bartender, who brought across a bottle of whiskey and two glasses. Jackson waited until the man had gone back behind the bar before pouring two drinks.

That done, he leaned closer to the sheriff, flinching at the smell of stale tobacco and whiskey on the lawman's breath.

His voice was little more than a hushed whisper when he eventually spoke.

'Quince, I think we may have a problem,' he said, 'or at least you may have a problem.'

Leroy took a slug from his glass and answered: 'If I've got a problem with something, Abe, then I can bet my life you've got the same. What's eating you?'

'Those two over in the corner, 'Jackson inclined his head in the direction of a distant table. 'Do you know them?'

Leroy emitted a contemptuous snort. 'I make it my business not to know anybody in this town. Makes the job easier. Anyway, what about them?'

The mayor tried to keep calm. He hated working alongside Quince Leroy but he had no choice. Alex McLagan ordered it.

'Who are they? What do you know about them?'

Leroy edged the mayor to one side to get a closer look at the two men in the corner.

'One's a guy called Duggan, Jack Duggan I think – got into town yesterday. He paid his money just the same as everybody else.'

'Any reward out on him?'

'None that's come through yet but the mail isn't too regular around here, Abe, you know that better than anybody.'

Jackson ignored the jibe – a clear reminder that Leroy knew all about the mail train robberies that had turned a former bank manager into an outlaw and landed him in Alvorado five years ago.

'What about the other man?'

Leroy leaned forward to get a better look at the second man.

'Nope, can't say I've seen him before, must have just got

into town today.'

'Then I suggest you go over there and find out more about him.'

Quince Leroy was sick of being ordered around by men like Jackson. Taking orders from the McLagans was bad enough but he was already well into plans for his own getaway, so obeying orders would soon be a thing of the past.

'Yeah, right, Mister Mayor. I'll talk to the man – if he's still in town tomorrow. Right now I've got a card game to finish.'

He got up and went back to the table where Harris and Sherwood were running out of patience.

Abe Jackson refilled his glass and studied the two strangers. He had a bad feeling about those two. Duggan had paid his money but, whatever his story, it was not backed up by any wanted poster. Quince had just taken his word and his money that he was who he said.

As for the other man, the nameless one, he too was a total stranger. And Jackson always worried when strangers arrived in Alvorado and did not go straight to the sheriff's office.

CHAPTER TEN

Roy McLagan was in a bad mood. He was always in a bad mood these days and the Mexican had a good idea why. The old man was putting pressure on him to marry the Bannon girl and Roy valued his freedom too much for that.

There was more to it, though. For months, maybe even a year, Roy had been hatching his plan for power.

'With the right men we can take over the whole territory, Mex. When the railroads come we'll take them over and the banks and the money men will follow. We'll turn this whole valley into an empire. We won't be answering to Washington or Mexico City or anywhere. We've got the guns and we can get the Indians and some of your men from south of the border to join us. All we need is for the old man to give the say so.' He paused there and then added: 'Or die.'

It was fanciful. Juan Herrera knew it would never happen. He knew that Roy did not have the wit to organize an orgy in a brothel, far less lead his own army into a battle that any sane man knew was impossible to win.

'We'll kill anybody who gets in our way. We'll burn out those homesteaders and farmers east of Alvorado. I tell you Mex. The name of Roy McLagan will cause Ulysses Grant and his bunch of spineless senators to wet their beds at night. That time is coming.'

Roy was drunk. And he was crazy. Juan Herrera had no intention of being around when Roy gathered his private army of misfits and added them to the group of killers who were paying the old man for protection from the law in Alvorado.

But now, as the pair of them sat opposite each other in the Big L House, winding down after the rest of the cowhands had drifted back to the bunkhouse, it was well after midnight and there was no sign of the old man. Or Lance.

'Where the hell can they be, Mex? Alex is way past chasing women and Lance – well he ain't got what it takes. Where are they?'

'My friend, you worry too much. They will be in the town in the Diamond saloon playing cards with some of the boys. It is normal.'

'Lance don't play cards, and the old man can't see far enough to tell what he's holding. You know, Mex, he thinks I don't know that his eyesight is failing. He thinks he can bluff it out but I've seen him trying to read the books. Even when he gives me the money to pay the hands he can't count the bills properly, giving me ones when they should be tens and fifties when they should be tens.

'The old man's day is gone.'

'*Sí*, my friend, but what can we do? We cannot go against Alex's will; we cannot get the men to go and fight without Alex saying the time is right. We cannot—'

He didn't finish. Roy jumped to his feet and hurled his glass into the fireplace. It shattered into tiny pieces.

'Cannot do this, cannot do that! That's all I hear from you, Mex. All the time it's Alex says, Alex thinks. Well Alex is an old man now. He can't tell us what we can do or when to do it. We've made plans and if we want to be big again we have to act now. We don't wait for Alex to decide. I'm sick of Alex.'

'But he is your father. He must have the final say on when we move.'

Roy slumped back into his seat; the threat of a violent outburst had gone and he sighed more in the frustration of hearing the truth than in any sense of defeat.

'Why, Mex?' he asked, his voice now more rational. 'Why must he always be the boss? We have been working for years to get the right men together; men who have been run off their own land under the orders of Washington. First it was Lincoln but when that southern loyalist Wilkes Booth put a bullet in him we were left with that bastard Andrew Johnson and his useless promises. Now it's Grant's turn to rub our noses in the dirt.

'We've got men willing to take us back to the days before the war, when the south was a Confederacy and Washington was in another country.

'This is why we started to grow the Big L and why we made Alvorado the town it is.'

Herrera nodded but said nothing. He no longer shared Roy's lust for war and blood. He remembered too well how his father was killed back in '48 when the two nations were at war; he had listened to stories of the Battle of the Alamo in 1836, and when the Yankees and the Rebels spent four years killing each other he felt it was exactly what they deserved.

But now, life was good. He was rich, thanks to Alex McLagan, and he had no intentions of following Roy into another pointless uprising that would be snuffed out before it even started.

Roy's obsession with his father's stories of the Mexican Wars and his exploits with Quantrill's Raiders during the

Civil War had turned his head and obsessed him for years, and Herrera felt that, at any time, his friend's anger would explode into a frenzy and he would lead his followers into a hopeless conflict. Soon it would be time for Jose to make a night-time disappearance and head south of the border.

Meanwhile, Roy slumped in his seat and said quietly to nobody in particular: 'Now – where the hell is my father when we need him to give us the order?'

Alex found sleep difficult, the increasing pains keeping him awake. He tried talking to his young son, Lance, who had stayed loyally at his hospital bedside.

Gathering all his stamina, the old man gripped Lance's hand and squeezed but there was little strength in it. His voice too was weak.

'Son, I want you to listen to me and I want you to heed what I'm saying.'

'Sure, Pa, I'm listening.'

Alex's grip on his son's hand tightened slightly, a confirmation that he believed the boy would digest what he was about to be told.

'I said listen, Lance, not interrupt,' said Alex but it was only as a friendly exchange between father and son. Lance fell silent but returned the strengthening of grip.

'I've done things I'm not proud of, boy, things I wish I had never done. Things that good folks will call bad things but I reckon I wouldn't have done if your ma had lived.

'I've killed people just for the hell of it or to get my own way. I had to do things some times to build up the Big L. Nobody just handed it to us. You were only a boy so you won't know what happened in those days.

'I fought people I didn't even know in wars I didn't understand.'

He paused briefly and Lance could see he was struggling

for breath but said nothing.

Eventually the old man went on: 'The time is coming for me to answer for all those bad things I've done. I'm ready to meet my maker and try to explain myself.'

There was another long silence, during which Lance felt the tears welling up inside.

'Don't say that, Pa,' he pleaded, 'you're going to be fine.'

Alex tried to smile.

'Don't worry, son. I'm settled. But I want you to make me a promise. You're not like me, Lance, you're a good son. I want you to promise me you'll stay just like you are.

'Now Roy – he's like me when I was young. Hot-headed, looking for trouble. He and that Mexican friend of his – they'll both finish their lives at the end of a rope or with a bullet in their back in some dark alley because of a woman and a jealous husband.

'He's not all bad, Lance. Remember that – he's your brother.

'I had hoped that when he married that pretty Amy Bannon he would settle down and he and Jim Bannon would run the Big L together. But that won't happen. Roy's no rancher. He's a gunfighter – and he sure as hell isn't the marrying kind.'

Alex suddenly started coughing and slumped back on to his pillows. Lance looked on anxiously but was relieved when his father regained his breath and started to speak again.

'When I'm gone I want you to get Jim Bannon over to run the Big L. You'll be in charge, but Jim knows ranching. You can learn a lot from him.'

The old man continued to lay out plans for the ranch's future after his death but eventually exhaustion got the better of him and he drifted off to sleep.

Lance had never asked his father about his business away from the ranch; nor had he challenged him about the reasons why Roy was always the centre of his affections. Was it because he was the first born? Or was it because he was so much like their father, while Lance had been the apple of his mother's eye?

It had never occurred to the younger brother until then that he and Roy may have had the same father but the fact they had different mothers, as Alex had remarried after the death of his first wife, meant that the resulting difference in their ages had left them belonging to different worlds.

Whatever the reason, the time had come for Lance to answer his father's call. But there was one more thing that the old man had to say.

'The man who helped you to bring me here, son.'

'His name's Jack Duggan. What about him, Pa?'

'I've been trying to think where I've seen him before and I've remembered. His name ain't Duggan. It's Brogan. Matthew Brogan.'

He paused to catch his breath before adding: 'I want you to find him, Lance. I want you to tell him to come back here. I have. . . .' a burst of coughing and spluttering interrupted his flow . . . 'I have something I want to say to him.'

'I've already told him you have thanked him for his help, Pa. There's no need to. . . .'

'Lance, I told you not to interrupt. It's not that, I've got to talk to him.'

'OK. I'll find him and I'll tell him. I'll be back tomorrow to see you . . . take you home, maybe.'

'Sure, son,' he said, before adding with a half-smile. 'Meantime, I won't be going anywhere.'

Lance checked with the hospital nurse that his father would be made comfortable and then headed out into the night.

It would be dawn before he reached the Big L. He knew the time was coming that he would have to confront Roy but he was already dreading a showdown.

There were six men in the small chapel but, apart from Jed Harding, the rest were strangers to Matt.

After Harding had called at the hotel, the two men had scoured the nearby farms and smallholdings in search of the kind of men they needed to carry out Harding's plan.

Don Barnes, a broad-shouldered bearded man in his forties, claimed he had been waiting for somebody to stand up to the McLagans and the men who had turned the town into an outlaws' refuge.

'You can count on me, stranger, and I reckon there are others around here who will be quick to join you,' he said.

Those others amounted to Tom Blake, who ran a one-man wheelwright and coach repair business but was eager 'to take those McLagans down a mite', and Caleb Thomas, whose wife had been living in fear ever since the men from the Big L started to stretch its boundaries.

The other stranger to Matt was Reverend Jonathon Elwell, who, if appearances were to be believed, had emerged from retirement. He was clad in the all-black garb of the small-town clergyman.

'We're going to need more men than this,' Matt said quietly, noticing the worried look on Harding's face. 'Six men – guns in the hands of small-time farmers and family men if you rule out the padre – plus us against the whole of the Big L don't make much sense to me.'

Jed tried a smile he hoped would be persuasive.

'You may be right, but I reckon not all the Big L cowhands will ride with the McLagans when the time comes. Some are genuine cattlemen, not gunfighters. And those that are on the run from the law won't want to join in a fight that has no profit in it.'

Matt was not convinced. From what he remembered they could be one and the same, and if their lifestyle was threatened they would be just as eager to use a gun.

'From what you've told me about last night they won't have Alex McLagan to lead them.'

Harding walked away and spoke to the clergyman.

'Listen, Reverend, if you want to leave now we won't think any less of you. This business is not for people in your line.'

Elwell put his hand on Harding's shoulder.

'You've seen what is outside in the churchyard, Mr Harding. My wife's gravestone. I'll stay and listen to what you have to say to these men, if you don't mind. And, whatever happens, you can count on me for more than a few words from a prayer book.'

Harding nodded.

'Right, men, let me tell you all why I wanted you to come here.'

'We want our town back,' Blake shouted, 'and if you and your friend here are going to help us get it let's hear what you've got to say.'

'Right now, there's only five of us – excuse me, Reverend, we'll leave you out of this for now – and that isn't going to be enough to stand up to the McLagans. So I want this meeting to be kept a secret until we can get the word out to other men you trust.

'Alex McLagan and his family have been running this town like it was their own private kingdom – '

'We know that,' barked Barnes, 'the question is, what can we do about it?'

'Please, Mr Barnes, let the man speak,' said Jonathon Elwell.

'Well, one thing in our favour is that the Big L won't

have Alex McLagan riding at the head of them like they have done. He's in hospital and, if Jack here is right, he could be close to death. Definitely not fit enough to ride.'

'I was the one who took him to hospital in Santa Rosa last night,' Matt said. 'I left him there with Lance but he looked in a sorry state.'

'That'll only make young Roy even more out of control,' Caleb interrupted.

'You won't have to worry about Roy,' Matt said. 'I can promise you that.'

The three farmers exchanged glances but said nothing. Who was this man who said his name was Jack Duggan. And who was this Harding who was giving the orders? A lawman from up north, the Reverend had said. But what was he doing in town?

'It's true we are going to need more men, especially men who can handle a gun, and we have to face up to the fact that not all of us will come out of it alive. But let me tell you what's at stake here.'

He studied the faces of the men in the room. They looked honest, eager to do what was right.

'It is two years ago that my brother was shot down when he got in the way of a bank robber's bullets. I was there and although I only got shot in the shoulder I promised my dying brother that I would hunt down the man who killed him.

'I became a lawman and came to Alvorado looking for his killer. My information is that the man I am looking for is here.' He waited for a response but all that came was silence.

He continued: 'With all the killing that's gone on in this place I am not surprised that you have not asked if I have him tracked down. The truth is it could be any one of a dozen wanted men who walk the streets of Alvorado as though they were untouchable.

'I'll find him but that's not why I got the reverend and Jack Duggan to round up as many men as we could muster to come here.

'The McLagan clan has got to be stopped, not only for you to reclaim your town, but to stop the threat of a return to bloodshed across the south.

'The war has been over for five years but there are some men who won't let it go. They still think of the north as the enemy and are ready to arm anybody of the same mind. But, even worse, when that fails they have the weapons and the money to rearm the Apaches and Comanche and rely on them to cause havoc in the southern states, forcing Washington to send troops.

'They are profiteers, men who make money out of wars, and they plan to turn to Mexico for help.'

Again there was only silence.

Harding pushed on: 'But worst of all for folks like yourselves, the McLagans, the Thomsons from Arizona and rebels from the Mexican-Franco war three years ago are thought to be planning to use the Big L as their base.'

'How do you know all this?' It was Barnes who butted in.

'Just believe it, I know. When the war ended we did not suddenly become one big happy family. We knew there would still be men, especially those who blamed Jefferson Davis for the south's defeat because of his bungling leadership, who wanted Lee to take over but he knew the war was over. He settled for a new United States of America. These men didn't. They have waited. They have robbed banks and trains until they have enough funds to pay for the weapons and the mercenaries to carry out their plans.

'That is why Alex McLagan and the others set up Alvorado – to bring in men like those who now run the town and others who claim to be cowhands at the Big L. We know that we have to stop them before they can gather all their forces and that time is now!'

The others eyed Harding with some suspicion. He had still not explained how he knew all this and until he did how could they put their trust in a man who had been in town for less than two days?

It was the reverend who spoke up for the rest.

'Mr Harding, we all of us have reasons not only to loathe but to fear men like Alex McLagan and his sons. They have been protecting thieves and killers all, but we believed it was to give them a hiding place from the law.

'Sheriff Quince Leroy and the Mayor Abe Jackson run things here for the McLagans.'

'But now somebody is going to stand up to them,' Jed interrupted. 'Now you know there is far more to the McLagans than just providing a killers' hideout. Jack, here and me, plus whoever you can round up, will be able to take care of the Big L crowd. What do you say?'

The reverend studied the rest of the men. They needed encouragement.

'I have been a man of God all my life. I have prayed for the day when Alvorado would be just like any other town, respectful of law and order, a place to bring up a family.'

He paused, studying the faces even more closely.

'But my wife is lying out there in her grave long before her time had come because nobody stood for what was right. And if good men like you stand by then the evil men of this world like the McLagans will go on ruining your lives.

'I have never taken up a gun in my life and it goes against everything I believe to start now but I will try to ease my conscience by praying that it is the right thing to do.'

Only Don Barnes remained doubtful. He strode forward until he stood less than a yard in front of Jed.

'You still haven't explained how you know all this, mister. Tell us.'

Jed thought for a moment, reluctant to give out any of the information the marshals' officers had gathered. He did not know these men well enough to trust them with the name of the man who had been feeding the intelligence to the service.

'Sorry, you'll just have to take my word for it.'

Barnes shook his head and backed away.

Caleb stepped up: 'But what's your plan, mister? How do you expect just a handful of us to stand up to a gang of killers? Do we just wait for McLagan's men to ride in?'

'No,' Jed said, waving his hand. 'If Jack is right about the state of Alex McLagan's health that could give us more time. Even a crazed kid like Roy won't act while his father's still in hospital.

'The best way to kill a poisonous snake is to cut off its head. Once that's done and one or two others take a bullet you can be sure the rest will saddle up and ride out. They won't hang around to be killed for somebody like McLagan. They're nobody's heroes.

'First you find the men – as many as you can muster – and get them here by dawn tomorrow. In the meantime, Jack and me will round up your sheriff and mayor and give the cells a couple of customers.

'When those two are locked up I'll ride out to meet the man who has been supplying us with our information. But one thing you have got to know – we will only get one chance at this. If we fail then Alvorado is lost forever and the McLagan men will start their own private war against anybody who gets in their way.'

Lance pulled up outside the sheriff's office, hitched the buggy to a post and went inside. He had been neglecting his duties as a deputy. He had never wanted the job, taking it only because his father had insisted. He was there solely to keep a watch on Quince Leroy.

'Somebody's got to watch that scheming crook,' the old man had said. 'I've never trusted him and Roy's far too busy to be able to take the job on.'

Too busy doing what? That had made Lance smile. Roy had a lot of interests but working on the ranch was not one of them, so when Lance arrived back from the hospital in Santa Rosa it hardly came as any surprise that his brother was nowhere to be found and none of the cowhands had any idea where he and that pig of a Mexican had gone.

The office was empty when Lance entered. He threw his hat on to the desk and slumped into the chair.

His father's illness had changed everything. The old man's health mattered more than how much Leroy was taking off the drifters and thieves who paid for protection from the law.

Lance pulled at the desk drawer. It was locked – as it was whenever Quince Leroy left the office. He had his secrets and Lance was convinced that if he could find their hiding place it would be enough to have his father run the sheriff out of town.

But what then? Who would be the next man to wear the tarnished star that was the badge of authority in this God-forsaken place?

Lance unsheathed his knife and slid the blade into the narrow gap between drawer and desk, listening for the click that released the lock. Sliding the drawer open, he delved inside and withdrew a sheaf of papers. Flipping through them, he was disappointed. He found the file contained nothing more than a pile of wanted posters. Most of the faces he recognized as men who had been to the ranch to see his father before moving into town. His father had never spoken to him about the visitors, though even as a growing youth he knew that some of the strangers who became familiar figures around the Big L were no more regular cowhands than he was.

A couple of envelopes from territory officials in Santa Fe containing requests for information regarding a group of escaped prisoners had gone unanswered, so Lance tossed them back into the drawer.

In a third file were newspaper cuttings that held Lance's interest. Brought up in a Confederate-supporting family, he had been too young to take more than an inquisitive son's interest in his father's stories of the war but once the hostilities were over he felt it was the right time to improve his education about the conflict that divided the nation.

He had read accounts in various journals, and here in the desk of the lawman's office in Alvorado were even more.

Both the Confederates and the Unionists claimed territorial rights over New Mexico and he already knew of the campaign of 1862 when Brigadier General Henry Hopkins Sidley led an invasion of the north of the territory in an attempt to gain control of the area including the Colorado Goldfields. The Battle of Glorieta Pass eventually ended the Confederates' grip on the territory.

Lance knew all this – but when he turned over one of the pages, his eyes dropped on a news item that made his blood run cold.

With growing alarm he read swiftly through the news report before stuffing it into his shirt pocket. Then, as he threw the rest of the papers back into the drawer, he spotted the key. Apart from the two cells at the back of the office there was only one other place that needed the use of a key – especially one kept hidden away in a locked drawer. The safe. That must be where Leroy kept his secrets.

Lance hurried across the room, knelt in front of the safe and tried the key. The door opened smoothly. Reaching inside, he withdrew a tin box but he never got the chance to look inside. He had been so engrossed in searching for something – anything – that would expose Quince Leroy he did not hear the movement from behind. The force of the gun butt crashing down on to his skull brought instant blackness.

Lance slumped forward, landing face down. His assailant stood over him and muttered: 'Crazy young fool, meddling where he ain't wanted.'

He holstered his gun and after taking what he had come for from the safe turned and left the way he had come – through the back door.

CHAPTER ELEVEN

Roy McLagan was in a good mood for a change and it was all because of the night spent in the bed of his Mexican girl. Her appetite knew no bounds and she fed Roy's ego with her coy, temptress looks. Hot-blooded – unlike his prim fiancée, Amy Bannon – Jacquinta made no demands outside the boudoir, and that too suited Roy. All he wanted was exclusive use of the girl's body and Jacquinta and her family knew better than to break that golden rule.

Whistling tunelessly, he dismounted outside the main house at the Big L, jogged cheerfully up the steps and went inside.

'Pa! Hey, Pa! You in there?'

There was no answer to his shout. He walked through to the rear verandah, where Gus, the old man the McLagans kept around to do all the cleaning and cooking, was sweeping away imaginary dust.

'Hey, old man, where is everybody? Mister Alex? Young Lance?'

Gus, a former slave in his late sixties, had been with the McLagan clan since before the boys were born, stopped to lean on his brush. He had never taken to Roy since he found him tormenting the family pup as a child. But he knew his place and remaining civil was a small price to pay for a peaceful life at the Big L.

'Sorry, Mister Roy, ain't seen nobody today,' he said as politely as he could manage. The sun was already rising over the range of hills to the east, so it was unusual to find the big house deserted. Amy or her father Jim Bannon were usually around by this time, keeping the old man talking to his heart's content.

Roy had arrived at the ranch in good spirits, content with the world, but that was fast disappearing. He had left Herrera back at the cantina to clear up the mess of the previous night's excesses, so now there was only Gus for company. Roy was not accustomed to talking to the hired help, so he went back inside the house and headed straight for the drinks cabinet. It was never too early for Alex McLagan's elder son to turn to a whiskey glass for comfort.

Grabbing the neck of the bottle, Roy slumped into the armchair that was usually almost exclusively occupied by his father and let his thoughts wander.

He treats it like some sort of throne, he mused bitterly, and treats us all like his subjects.

Roy had been spending a lot of time thinking about his father in the past few days. He was getting too old to make plans for the future; but it was not his future, it belonged to younger men – men like Roy and Mex.

There was no place in Roy's future for the Bannons. They could keep their little plot of land and their shack of a house, and Amy could carry on feeding the chickens and going off for her private picnics.

Roy had bigger plans. He took a long swig from the whiskey bottle, got up from his seat and went up the staircase to his private room. Once there he slid a battered old case from beneath the bed, flipped it open and pulled out a neatly wrapped bundle.

From inside the package he withdrew a bloodstained

Confederate flag, a battered notebook and an old handgun with the initials WQ scratched on the handle . . . the initials of his father's great friend and colleague in the Partisan Rangers.

Roy read through the well-thumbed pages for the hundredth time in an attempt to relive the stories of his father's exploits alongside William Quantrill.

He cursed when he read again the news about the Confederate government that had given Quantrill a field commission withdrawing their support, meaning that by 1864 Quantrill's men had spread themselves far and wide.

Then came news of Quantrill's death in a Union ambush. Ray read through the scrawled entry his father had made in the notebook.

At the top of the page was the date – May, 1865.

Lee's surrender at Appomattox last month sickened Captain Bill and the rest of us felt the same. We were down badly on numbers and Lee had told us the war was over. We were caught in a Union ambush at Wakefield Farm and the blue jackets shot him in the back. Even then they couldn't kill him – they had to wait until they got him into one of their hospitals in Kentucky where he died. Those bastards did for him but they didn't do for his spirit. We will keep his memory alive.

Roy remembered how each year his father had left the ranch in the hands of Jim Bannon to go on regular reunions of the survivors of Quantrill's gang. For Alex McLagan and the men who had ridden with them and their friends, the name of William Quantrill would never die.

But that was not in Roy's plans as he snapped the notebook shut and returned it with the handgun and flag to its hiding place under the bed.

He had other ideas about the name of Quantrill. From now on another name would replace it – McLagan's Marauders would live on long after William Quantrill was forgotten.

The plans were almost in place; he could have men from across the territory ready in days but right now his concern was for the whereabouts of his father.

Where the hell was the old man? And where was Lance? The kid was never around when he was needed.

An hour later Roy, who had already drunk half a bottle of whiskey, was still waiting for either his brother or his missing father to put in an appearance, while three miles away, in a quiet clearing to the south side of Alvorado, two men were in deep discussion and Roy McLagan was the main topic of that conversation.

Jed Harding had listened while he heard of Alex McLagan's rapidly fading health and Roy's ambitions to take control of the whole territory and beyond.

'Alex is head of the McLagan family in name only now,' Jed was told. 'He has been sick for a long time but he has tried to keep it from everybody. Roy is too full of his own ideas and self-importance to notice that his father is sick. He and that Mexican Herrera run the place like it was their own empire, though they have no interest in ranching.

'Power and property are what they are after. They have hired guns willing to join Roy when he gives the word. You'll find out who they are when you and this new friend of yours take over the sheriff's office from that crook Leroy.

'Young Lance is the only one at the Big L with a shred of decency left but he is powerless to do anything. It's not that he's afraid of his brother, he's just too loyal to the family.'

Harding did not interrupt as the other reported what he had learned . . . how Roy planned to get together enough men to take over the town and move across maybe into Texas, where he claimed support of other disillusioned southerners. Then into Arizona.

'They say they are sick of being told by Washington how to lead their lives – the north on one side and the Mexicans on the other. And then there's the Apache.

'From what I hear, Roy is just waiting for the old man to hand over the Big L before he makes a move. It can't be soon enough for him.

'He's crazy though he doesn't say much when I'm around – he knows how I feel about him, but some of the cowhands think I am part of the plan so there's some loose talk.

'As soon as I know what the plans are I'll get word to you. Now that you're here it saves me the trouble of sending those messages up to the State Department

'All I can say now is that his first move will be to take over the town, so I reckon you should get your men ready for anything.

'Oh, and there's one other thing.' He reached inside his shirt and handed Harding a neatly folded sheet of paper. 'I think this is what you've been waiting for. It arrived in the mail yesterday.'

Jed unfolded the paper, read the contents and allowed himself a half-smile.

'Thanks,' he said, 'this should do the trick.'

The two men shook hands and Jed headed back to town. The other stood and watched until Harding disappeared from view. Then he turned and walked back towards the small house. He had just reached the steps when the young girl emerged from inside the house.

'Who was that, Dad?'

He put his arm around his daughter's shoulder as they went back into the house.

'Just somebody your brother once knew.'

He hated the idea of lying to his daughter but if it helped to keep her out of the clutches of Roy McLagan it would be worth any brief spell of hurt she would feel when her cheating fiancé was locked away. And he could stop leading his double life . . . rancher or government agent – Jim Bannon could make his choice.

Lance opened his eyes and tried to get to his feet. But his head ached and his legs refused to take his weight and buckled under him. He eventually managed to stagger to his chair and slump across the desk. The huge egg-shaped lump on the back of his head was further evidence of the attack.

He tried to gather his thoughts. Where was Quince Leroy? Who had entered the office and attacked him?

He stared down at the open door of the safe and there were papers scattered across the floor. The tin box he had been about to open was now lying upturned and empty in the far corner of the room.

The throbbing in Lance's head grew worse and when he tried to move the pain was so fierce it forced him back into his chair. He closed his eyes and fingered the lump. As he moved his hand away, it brushed against his shirt. The newspaper cutting was still there.

Gingerly, he removed it from his pocket, unfolded it and carefully flattened it on the desk. He studied it again, only this time more closely.

It was cut from a copy of the Santa Fe Bulletin and it was dated almost a year earlier.

The heading read: JUDGE JAILED ON CORRUPTION AND BRIBERY CHARGES.

Underneath was the report.

Henry Coburn, who served as a circuit judge for fifteen years until his retirement, is today commencing a five-year jail sentence after being found guilty of accepting payments in the form of bribes during his term in office.

The legislature is now investigating the outcome of a number of cases heard by the judge, now resident in Santa Fe.

The Bulletin understands that evidence of corruption was discovered in a number of books taken from Judge Coburn's home and involved more than $50,000 of payments during a ten-year period.

Henry Coburn, whose wife is the sister of leading New Mexico rancher Alex McLagan, has been a leading figure in Santa Fe political life for several years and he called upon Mr McLagan as a character witness during his trial.

However, despite the support of his brother-in-law and several other prominent members of the city council, Coburn was found guilty of corruption and bribery. We understand that detectives will be investigating up to thirty cases that came before Coburn over a five-year period.

The Bulletin was informed that it would take several months, perhaps years, to determine the number of men and women wrongfully imprisoned by Coburn.

Lance folded the cutting and put it back in his shirt.

He had little knowledge of his uncle Henry, having met him on only two or three occasions when he was an impressionable youngster. An uncle who was a judge – that was important to a studious boy like Lance but now, in his shirt pocket, was evidence that his uncle had put innocent men behind bars. Or even worse, there were those he had sent to the gallows.

Now, though, Lance had more important things on his

mind. Who had attacked him? Where was Quince Leroy? And was Roy back at the house? He had to be told about the old man's health.

He got up from his chair and was heading out of the office when the front door opened and two men walked in.

One was the man who had helped get his father to hospital in Santa Rosa. He said his name was Jack Duggan. The other was a total stranger.

CHAPTER TWELVE

The kid was a fool. Sticking his nose in where it was not wanted. He would have a headache but he would get over it.

'Maybe I should have hit him harder,' Quince Leroy said, thinking aloud as he pulled his horse to a halt at the foot of the gulch. He removed his hat and ran his arm across his brow. The sun was already high. It was going to be another hot day.

It was a good time to get away. He had a long, hard ride ahead before making it to California, out of the reach of the McLagans once and for all . . . along with the $5,000 he had taken from the office safe.

He had earned that money down the years he had been running the town for Alex.

He nudged his mount slowly forward. He knew he would have been spotted by the men high on the hillside but their job was to stop people from going into town, not those who were leaving. Confidently waving his hat in mock salute to the two guards, he urged the horse into a canter and out on to the open plain that would take him north, then west where he would be a free man.

Leroy never took another stride to freedom. Instead a rifle bullet ripped into his back and then, as he fell from the saddle, another caught him in the throat, ending his life in an instant.

Mitch Buller grinned and lowered the rifle.

He turned to his companion and spat some tobacco chew into the parched earth.

'Roy was right, Mex. Old Quince couldn't be trusted. The boss knew he'd make a run for it one day.'

'Yes, Mitch, Roy was right.' He didn't add that Leroy would not be the last to make a break from the grip of McLagan.

'Wonder where he was headed,' Mitch mused. 'I guess we'll never know. Let's get down there and pick up the body, you never know what we might find in his pockets. I like the look of that sorrel Quince has been riding.'

The two men made their way down the slope, Mitch chatting endlessly but Herrera wasn't listening. He was deep in thought – and those thoughts had nothing to do with Quince Leroy or his horse.

He was already planning his own getaway.

Matt grinned at the look of surprise on Lance's face as the two men entered the sheriff's office. He turned towards his companion.

'Lance, I want you to meet a friend of mine, Jed Harding. Jed, this is Lance McLagan.'

Lance got to his feet but it was an effort and he had to grip on to the table to stop himself from falling. He slumped back into his chair.

'Sorry,' he said feebly, 'as you can see we've had a. . . .'

'You've had a crack on the head,' Matt interrupted, 'and it looks to me as though somebody has emptied your safe.'

He looked around the room.

'Where's our friend, the sheriff?'

Lance shook his head but that too hurt.

'I don't know where he is, but I'm his deputy. Can I help?'

It was Harding who leaned forward. 'You sure can, young feller. You can hand over your star. From here on, you won't be needing it.'

Lance looked over the stranger's shoulder at Matt, hoping for an explanation.

'Sit down, Lance. Harding here is a federal lawman. He's taken me on as his deputy and we are here to see that Alvorado gets a good clean up.'

'I don't understand.'

'Sure you do, kid,' Harding interrupted. 'But maybe I should explain it to you again.

'I came to this town looking for the man who killed my brother but that was only part of it. The rest was to report what I found in Alvorado and make recommendations to my bosses back in Denver.'

He paused before adding: 'You look worried, son. Why can that be?'

'Listen, mister, I don't know what you're talking about. What has Denver, Colorado, got to do with what happens in New Mexico?'

'Maybe they are just being real neighbourly and looking out for their friends. I'll explain it to you,' Harding said, losing patience. 'The McLagan reign is over. Alvorado is no longer your family's private property to do with what you and the rest of the Big L are planning. There are enough good folk around here to stop you from running them out of their homes. They just needed somebody to tell them. Your brother and his gang are planning to burn down every house in the valley and – '

'You're crazy!' Lance snapped, suddenly getting to his feet, ignoring the searing pain from the crack over the head. 'I don't know what in hell's name you're talking about but right now I don't even care. My father is lying in a hospital bed in Santa Rosa probably close to death' – he shot a glance at Matt – 'ask him if you don't believe me. I've told you I don't know where the sheriff has gone. I don't care much about that either. I need to find my brother to tell him what's happened to our father. As for you cleaning up this hellhole of a town, I wish you all the luck.'

He pulled the deputy badge from his shirt, ripping the pocket, and threw it on the desk.

He made for the door but Jed stepped in front of him, halting his stride. He thrust a poster in his face.

'Do you know this man?'

Lance backed away to study the picture.

He shook his head.

'No, I don't know him. Is he the man you're here to find?

'This is the man I came looking for,' Jed said, his anger rising. 'His name is Ray Shelby. He killed my brother.'

Jed stuffed the picture back in his shirt pocket. If Lance McLagan did not recognize the man in the picture then the search would go on. Shelby was in Alvorado – Jed was convinced of that. But where was he hiding out? Where better for a coyote to hide than in a pack of coyote? The same went for a killer like Shelby. He could go unnoticed in a town full of killers and bank robbers.

He stepped aside and let Lance leave the office. Despite the heat outside the younger McLagan brother felt a cold sweat brought on by what the stranger had told him. He knew that Roy had been doing business with the comancheros, a group of Mexicans who in turn traded with the Great Plains Tribes including the Comanche in northern New Mexico and West Texas.

But he also knew that things had changed since the end of the War Between the States. The comancheros had moved from trading in flour and tobacco and manufactured goods to supplying firearms and ammunition to aid in their fight against the US Government.

Lance had not wanted to know but now he could hardly ignore it. His father was dying and his younger brother was planning a range war.

Roy McLagan saw himself as the leader of a new breed of warmongers. With Herrera at his side and some of the Big L ranch hands and hordes of whiskey-fueled Indians forming his private army there was nothing to stop him.

He had to be stopped. But how? There was no reasoning with Roy but he had to try – not for his brother's sake, or even his own, but for Amy.

He decided to leave the buggy where it was, collect a horse from the stables at the end of the street and head out to the ranch. Roy had to be found and told of their father's state of health. Maybe a pang of conscience might cause him to at least delay his plans.

Lance left town at full speed, watched by just two people . . . the men who had taken over the job of restoring law and order to the town built in Hell.

Roy McLagan's temper had not improved with the passing of the hours he had spent waiting for Lance or his father to put in an appearance. Mex and the others had long since left the house and were out on the range. It was only when he saw his brother approaching at high speed that he finally found a target for his anger.

He waited for Lance to dismount and head up the steps before yelling: 'Where in Hell have you been? And where is the old man?'

Roy had always been able to frighten his younger brother. Ever since they were kids Roy, bigger and four years older, had been a bully, throwing his weight about and picking on the young sibling every chance he got, even teasing him in front of his friends.

But not today. Lance would not be cowed; there was nothing Roy could do or say that would frighten him.

Without answering, he brushed his brother aside and marched into the house. He threw his hat on to a chair and headed straight for the drinks table. Lance had never been a heavy drinker but right now a large glass of whiskey was what he needed.

He gulped it down and turned to see Roy standing in the doorway. He was still angry.

'I asked you a question, little brother. Where have you been? And where's Pa?'

'That's two questions, Roy. And right now I don't feel like answering either of them.'

Roy marched forward and for a moment Lance thought he was going to throw a punch. Instead, he just snarled: 'Don't get clever with me, young Lance. You ain't big enough to try that.'

Lance emptied his glass. 'That's it with you, Roy. Big enough is all that matters. Big with your fists, big with your guns and big with your mouth. That's your answer for everything. Well, they won't get you out of this trouble.'

Roy leaned forward, grabbed his brother by the shirt and shook him violently.

'What you saying? What trouble are you talking about? I ain't going to ask you again, kid. If I have to beat it out of you, then I will.'

Lance pushed his brother's hands away and moved towards the drinks table to refill his glass. He slid into the chair that his father had been slumped in when he had been rushed into hospital the night before.

He looked his brother full in the face. There was no hint of fear now.

'All my life I have tried to like you, Roy,' he said, his voice level, his tone measured. 'To have an older brother I could admire. You were always Pa's favourite. I knew that, but that is fine by me. You were older, his first son. But I was wrong and now I know it.

'You asked me where's Pa. If you spent more time here instead of drinking with your Mexican friends and their women, you would know that last night the old man's heart almost gave out. I rushed him to hospital in Santa Rosa, where he is now.'

He waited for his brother to interrupt but Roy said nothing.

'For all I know he may be dead but isn't that what you have been waiting to hear?'

Roy snapped and, fists clenched, he edged forward.

'Listen, kid, the old man will die sooner or later. His days are over. It's time for him to step aside and leave it up to people like me. He's gone soft and now you tell me he's in a hospital bed. Well, you're right. I won't be doing any crying.'

Lance gulped down another drink and stared at his brother. It was all there in Roy's face – a cold hatred that had festered for as long as he could remember.

Then came the question he needed answering, although when it came it sounded as though he was hearing it being said by another voice.

'What about Amy?'

For a moment Roy said nothing. Then, in the rapid change of mood Lance had come to expect, he broke into a fit of laughter.

'The Bannon girl? She's all yours, brother. Why do you think I kept her around? It sure as hell wasn't for what she was offering. It was because I knew you wanted her and I enjoyed seeing you make a fool of yourself. I've watched you drooling all over her ever since you knew what to use it for.

'Little Miss Proper, saving herself for big bad Roy while all the time you were trying to get into her knickers.'

Lance lost control, hurling his glass at his brother, but Roy saw it coming and ducked to one side. Still laughing almost hysterically, he dived forward, landing on top of the younger man. The chair crashed over and both men landed in a heap in the corner of the room. Glasses and bottles smashed and the table toppled over and clattered into the wall.

Lance let out a yell as Roy's elbow caught him full in the face and sent blood spurting from his nose. The pair grappled on the floor, rolling out on to the verandah at the rear of the house before scrambling to their feet to face each other.

Barely a word passed between them as they slugged it out in the dust at the back of the house, Lance ignoring the pain from the blow he had taken in the office.

They exchanged punches but in the end there could only be one winner of a straight fist fight between the brothers and they both knew it. Growing hate would not save Lance against the bigger, stronger, older man who knew all the tricks of a bar room brawl.

Lance got lucky with a swinging blow that caught Roy full on the jaw, sending him spinning backwards more in shock than any threat of serious injury. He was still smiling when he got to his feet.

'Well, Lance, I'll say this for you – you found yourself some guts from somewhere when it comes to fighting for a lady's honour. Except you're too late – I've already taken that. Gladly offered, happily taken.'

'You're a liar, Roy. A filthy stinking liar.'

'Oh, maybe, maybe not. But you ain't so sure, little

brother. You ain't so sure.'

'Shut up! Shut up, or—'

He suddenly found himself reaching for his gun. In an instant it was in his hand and he was pointing it at his brother's chest.

Roy also reached down but the holster was empty. His gun had fallen out during the fight.

'Slow down, brother. Take it easy. You wouldn't shoot down an unarmed man. Not even me.'

Lance felt himself shaking. He was angry enough to do just that. Kill his own brother. But if he did he would be no better than Roy or any of the others.

'You want to try me, Roy?' he snapped. 'There's nobody here – just you and me. Who would know it wasn't self-defence? You were drunk, came in here, fighting, out of your mind with grief over Pa. What do you think, Roy? Why would folk not believe me, the quiet, studious one of the McLagan family?'

'OK, I'm leaving here, Lance. I'm going to walk slowly away, get on my horse and ride out. In a day or two I'll come back and we can talk about this. What do you say?'

'It would be better if you didn't come back at all, but maybe in a day or two. Pa could be back by then and we can talk.'

Roy lowered his hands. 'Fine, that's fine.'

He turned away and started to walk to the corral but Lance called after him: 'I won't forget what you said about Amy. I won't forget it.'

He watched his brother mount up and ride off into the heat of the day. He knew there would be no going back, no reconciliation. The damage had been done long before the fight, and even before he had besmirched Amy's name.

It had been done when that federal marshal Jed Harding had shown him the picture of the man who he believed to be a killer called Ray Shelby and destroyed the last fragments of family loyalty.

The first flames over Alvorado lit up the black skies of eastern New Mexico that same night. Caleb Thomas could only watch, his arm around his crying wife, as his house burned to the ground and five torch bearers rode off in the direction of the Big L.

Roy McLagan had not waited for the death of his father to carry out the first part of his rule of terror.

CHAPTER THIRTEEN

The church bell rang for the first time in three years but it was not to summon the good folk of Alvorado to prayer, although Matt Brogan knew it was the day of reckoning for the town and its people.

The previous night's blaze and the slaughter of a dozen steers had reduced Caleb Thomas and his wife Lettie to a state of homelessness and poverty.

'There were five of them. Masked riders came and dragged us out of the house and forced us to watch as they burned our home to the ground. They told us to make sure that the rest of the families in the valley knew what would happen to them if they did not pack up their things and leave. Then they rode off in the direction of the McLagan spread.'

It was a story that brought back the horrors of that fateful night of three years earlier when Matt's family had been the victims whose house had been burned and his wife and son murdered.

Like everybody else, Matt was convinced that the raid on Caleb's farm was the work of Roy McLagan and his buddies. His father was in hospital two hours' ride away in Santa Rosa, maybe close to death; Lance was not capable of the crimes and Roy's plans to build his own empire were known throughout the district.

There were twenty men and six women in the small church room, all angry and ready to risk their lives to defend their homes. But Jed and Matt both knew that anger and good intentions would not be enough to turn a small group of peace-loving farmers into a fighting force against the guns of the Big L.

Reverend Elwell called on another of the homesteaders, Bill Coley. A thickset, big-muscled man in his forties, he had moved into the area with his wife and son at the end of the war, which had left him with a leg wound that forced him to walk with a limp.

'Ever since we got here we've had trouble from the Big L crowd and we've all been too frightened to do anything about it. All of us. Now we've got somebody offering to help.'

He waved his hand in the direction of Jed and Matt.

'These two men have nothing to gain by helping us. They don't belong here. They could both ride out and forget all about us and leave us to whatever the McLagans have got planned. Let's hear them out.'

There was an awkward silence before Coley added: 'Joey here's my son.' He put his arm around the shoulder of a young boy of about 10 years old – not unlike Toby, as Matt remembered his own son. 'I don't want him to grow up in a place where he can't walk down the street in safety. We all know what goes on in Alvorado since Abe Jackson became mayor and the McLagans gave that crook Quince Leroy the sheriff's star. If we don't give these two men a chance we can go on living in fear. And that's exactly what we would deserve.'

Jed and Matt had spent the early part of the day talking over their plans. News of the fire had spread fast, though many of the neighbours had already spotted the flames when the blaze was at its height around midnight.

'Yeah, what you got in mind, mister?' another of the farmers shouted from the back of the room, and his call brought cheers of approval from those standing close by.

Reverend Elwell called for order and Jed stepped up on to the improvised pulpit. Looking down on the gathering, he could only hope that their desire to rid Alvorado of the McLagan grip was as strong as his own.

'I need five or six volunteers to join us' – hands went up before he could say any more – 'but I need good riders who can handle a gun.' The arms remained in the air.

'But I don't want any family men; no fathers with young kids or menfolk whose wives may be wondering if they will ever see their man again.'

A couple of hands were lowered but Jed pressed on and counted the raised arms.

'That leaves ten volunteers. Good. Now let me tell you what we are planning. If you are all still interested after that I will make the choice.

'Caleb's house and stock was only the first. You are all targets for the Big L bunch but if we wait for them to pick you off one by one, we will never stop them. We cannot watch every farm all the time, there are not enough of us and we have no way of knowing where they will hit next.'

'And how we gonna stop them?' somebody shouted from the back of the room. Jed reckoned it was the same voice as before.

'We're going to hit them before they hit us.'

There was a stunned silence before the first man yelled: 'You crazy? Eight or ten men against the McLagan crowd of maybe thirty or forty, most of them already killers.'

'All I ask is that you trust us,' Jed said, once the muttering among the doubters had died.

'There is only one street in and out of town. Those of

you who are left behind will barricade both ends. Maybe those barricades and your guns won't be needed but if they are you will still have a fighting chance.'

The men started talking among themselves and Matt began to wonder whether the townsfolk would go for a plan they knew nothing about other than the fact that two strangers were leading them.

Eventually, the reverend spoke up for the rest.

'One thing puzzles me and probably everybody here, is just how are we going to stop the cutthroats and murderers who are already here from attacking us from within?'

'I guess you will just have to trust me on that too, padre.'

Again, the man at the back of the room was quick to join in.

'Seems to me we're putting a hell of a lot of trust in you, mister. If your clever plan fails you can just ride away and leave us to the McLagans, who will be worse than ever.'

Jed held up his hand. 'What's your name, mister?'

'Richard Ellis. I own the place down by the stream, Sundown Creek. Old man McLagan would like to get his hands on my place for sure.'

'Well, Richard, let me tell you and everybody else here. I won't be riding anywhere if I fail you. Just like all the volunteers I'm picking – I'll be dead.'

There was a murmur of approval from the crowd and Ellis, irritated at the lack of support for his case against the two strangers, slid quietly into the corner of the room, muttering something about talking big. Nobody was listening. The rest of the crowd had been won over. They were ready to back the federal agent who was prepared to put his own life at stake to help the town.

'Reverend Elwell has volunteered to take charge of the barricading, which will start at dawn tomorrow.'

'Who not sooner – why not now?' somebody shouted.

'Because that would be like sending a message straight to the Big L to let them know we are expecting them. All Mayor Jackson would do is send a rider out to the McLagan spread and they would be all over you like a plague of locusts.'

There were more nods of agreement before Jed went on: 'Some of you know that I came to this town to find the man who killed my brother during a bank raid two years ago. His name is Ray Shelby. I have here a sketch of him taken off a wanted poster. I believe it is a good likeness.'

He reached into his shirt pocket and withdrew the picture he had shown Lance McLagan.

'I hope one of you may have seen him about town.'

He shook it open and handed it to Reverend Elwell who, without a glance, passed it on to the nearest man.

He needed just one quick look to identify the dark, scowling features on the poster.

'You won't have to look too far for him, Mr Harding. This guy ain't known around here as Ray Shelby. This is Roy McLagan.'

CHAPTER FOURTEEN

Matt Brogan rode alone to the hospital in Santa Rosa, leaving Jed in town to help the preacher organize the defences.

The revelation that they were both chasing the same killer and that that man was planning to take over the whole valley and much of the territory of New Mexico had forced Matt to take a fresh look at his plans.

Roy McLagan had killed his wife and son; he had gunned down Jed Harding's brother during a bank raid and Harding was the law. There was a lot of persuading to do before they came face to face with the Big L bunch and Matt was no longer certain that the plan they had devised would work.

The men Harding chose would be willing enough and there was no doubting their bravery but they were not gunfighters, so everything depended on the success of Matt's visit to the man he had vowed to kill but now must turn to for help.

It was mid-afternoon when he reached the small hospital, so already time was short. As he dismounted, Matt was not surprised to see a buggy tied up close by. Lance was already there.

But he was not alone. Alex McLagan was propped up on a bunch of pillows and his bed was flanked by two visitors, his son Lance and the pretty young girl Matt had rescued from a long walk home two days earlier, Amy Bannon.

The old man was pale and he looked even weaker than when he had been brought to the hospital. When he looked up to see Matt enter the room he nodded. Neither friendly nor hostile – just acknowledgement that the man he had sent for had agreed to come.

The girl, too, greeted him with a nod.

'Mr Duggan,' she said simply.

'The name's Brogan, miss. Matthew Brogan.'

Lance looked away but Matt noticed that his cheek was swollen and there was a deep bruise around his left eye. If Lance had won the fight, Matt would not have liked to see the state of the loser.

'Good of you to come, Brogan, and thanks for helping Lance to get me here. For what it is worth, you probably saved my life.'

'I don't feel any better for that,' Matt said bitterly. 'Maybe you won't want these young people to hear what I have to say or why I am here.'

McLagan raised his hand in an effort to stop Matt saying anything further. It was a feeble gesture but Matt fell silent.

'If you had arrived an hour earlier you would have heard me tell Lance and Amy why you came to Alvorado. I told them what happened three years ago, how I bribed my sister's husband to make sure you were convicted for killing your family. I did it to save my son from the gallows, Brogan – any father would have done the same.'

Matt's hands were at his side but he felt his jaw tighten and his fists clench as he tried to control his desire to reach out and strangle what was left of life out of the old man.

Instead, he showed his contempt by snarling: 'God may forgive you, McLagan, but I won't. Don't try to justify what you did to me and my family by blaming it on some crooked judge. You and your son killed them and put me in the penitentiary to pay for it.'

'We were drunk,' the old man said feebly and then repeated it even more quietly. 'We were drunk.'

Amy stood up and leaned over to mop the old man's brow.

'Mr Brogan, can't you see he is ill. What's done is done.'

'Not just ill, Brogan,' McLagan interrupted. 'I'm dying. It's too late to put things right with you and being sorry for what happened is no help. Killing me would only shorten my life by a few weeks, maybe days. There's nothing more I can do.'

'You're wrong. You know I came here to kill you and your son and that Mexican but, if as you say you are dying, I'd gain nothing by killing you. Right now, I'm here to keep you alive, at least for one more day.'

The other three exchanged puzzled glances.

Matt studied the man in the bed as if seeing him for the first time as an old and frail figure waiting for death. What help could this man offer even if he agreed?

'I need your help,' he said at last. 'I'll never forgive you for what you did but you might just be the kind of man who would like to meet his maker on good terms. Your conscience can never be clear but that's a price that your soul will have to pay. Before that time comes you still have the chance to put a stop to a whole lot of killing.'

McLagan eased himself into a sitting position. 'Tell me what you want me to do.'

Matt explained what he expected of the Big L owner. But he did not point out that, whatever happened, the

McLagan family would be short of one son before it was all over.

The Diamond Bar was filling up rapidly when Alex McLagan, with the help of his younger son, walked in. Matt was close behind.

McLagan's appearance had the effect of a huge curtain of silence being thrown over the room. All eyes turned towards the man in the grey town suit and the white hat.

Lance and Amy had worked wonders on the old man's appearance since they had taken him from the hospital that afternoon. He had to be presented to the saloon crowd as a picture of good health – a man still in control of everything that happened in and around the town of Alvorado. If the plan failed at the first hurdle then the burning and killing would spread across the whole valley. Roy McLagan would not be happy until he had driven every farmer out of the territory or put them in an early grave.

'Mr McLagan, welcome.'

It was Rafferty, the long-serving Irish bartender, who broke the silence. He had known McLagan longer than most of the people around town and had always looked upon the old man as strong but fair with anybody who did not try to cheat him.

'We don't see you in here too often. What'll be your pleasure?'

McLagan waved the man away.

'Later, Patrick.' He had other things on his mind ahead of his next glass of whiskey. Brogan had left him with a simple choice – either help to stop what could be a range war and the threat of a massacre or go to his grave a broken man loathed by everybody who knew him, unmourned even by his young son, who now stood at his side offering support.

There was still an uneasy silence as McLagan prepared to make the speech. His voice had to be strong – to carry the command he had shown since he opened the streets of the town to those men with money to pay for a safe hide-away.

Killers, bank robbers, army deserters – Alex McLagan had not concerned himself with their crimes, only that they had enough money to pay for their sanctuary.

But now it was all over and it was McLagan's duty to make the speech. Not a Lincoln-style Gettysburg address or even a sniveling Robert E Lee surrender apology but he had to convince these men that Alvorado was no longer a safe place to hide.

He was used to barking orders and for those orders to be obeyed. During the war, then as owner of the Big L and father of two sons, he was the man with the voice of authority. But this was different. Now he was under orders from somebody else – orders to call the biggest bluff of his life. Brogan had told him what was to be said but it was up to him to convince the motley gathering of law-breakers that Alvorado was no longer safe. It was time to get away.

Brogan had delivered his warning like a man who held all four aces.

'You're already dying, McLagan, so it is too late for me to get the satisfaction of killing you for what you did but unless you want to take your sons with you then you'll get the message across.

'The people in this town have been doing your bidding and obeying your orders, running scared from your gang for too long. They want their town back.'

Alex McLagan coughed. The pain was increasing and he was struggling to stay steady on his feet. He looked around the room – maybe he should have taken that drink after all.

He recognized many of the men at the card tables and the roulette wheel.

Suddenly one of them got up from his seat. Max Benson was a thick-set, pasty-skinned man with deep set eyes, with a three-day growth of greying beard. His face was locked in a permanent twisted scowl. He had been in Alvorado for only two days and he was seeing Alex McLagan for the first time. He had expected something more than the frail-looking figure whose name had been treated with respect and admiration by everybody who spoke about him.

Benson, bank robber and killer, was not impressed.

'You got something to say, mister, only you're interrupting my winning streak here. So could you hurry on with it?'

It was the sort of challenge that Alex McLagan, even in his present state, could not ignore.

'And who are you?'

'The name's Max Benson – I got here two days ago. Your man the sheriff took the cash.'

Alex allowed himself a short smile. Two days – $200, if Quince Leroy had done his job. He scanned the room but there was no sign of Leroy. Where was he? Why wasn't he here?

'Well, Benson. I think you should pick up your winnings and ride out of here. And that means all of you.

'Most of you men came here because it made you safe from the law. That was because of me and the Big L. Well, now it's over.'

Again it was Benson who stepped forward.

'You've taken our money, McLagan. We paid you to keep the law out of town.'

'Yeah, what do you say to that, Alex? You now want to run us out of town?'

A small group at the roulette wheel laughed but the mood was turning ugly.

Alex McLagan suddenly found himself gasping for breath and a retching coughing attack forced him to lean on his son for support.

'You've gotta tell 'em, Mr Brogan,' Lance said, helping his father to a chair. 'You can see he can't do it. He's tried.'

Matt could see that the old man was in no state to carry on with the speech that would clear the streets of Alvorado but these men had to be told. If they believed what Matt had to say then the odds of restoring the town to a safe home for law-abiding citizens would shorten.

He faced the crowd of men who were now arguing among themselves, with Benson clearly stirring things up.

He had to shout to make himself heard.

'Listen, you men. Alex McLagan got out from his sick bed so that he could warn you that this town is no longer a safe place. By dawn tomorrow Alvorado will be under martial law. President Grant has ordered troops to move down from Fort Sedgewick in Colorado to clean up this part of the territory.'

There was a stunned silence before somebody shouted: 'Who are you, mister? And how do you know all this?'

It was the cue for Matt to play his part. He reached in his pocket and pulled out a sheet of paper and waved it above his head.

'This telegraph came early today. It reads: Confirm troops have left Fort under command of Captain Joseph Morgan with orders to put town under Martial Law. Signed General P.D. Myers.'

Matt folded the paper and returned it to his pocket. 'I know Morgan. He'll come heavily armed and ready for any opposition. He's a shoot to kill man who doesn't ask questions, as the Indians found out when a thousand of them, Cheyenne, Arapaho and Sioux, raided Julesburg back in '65. Then, after the war, Morgan led the army's protection of the Overland Trail. He's a man who likes the taste of blood.

'He'll have maybe two hundred or more troopers with him to carry out his orders and I . . . .'

'Hold it right there, mister!'

The interruption came from a tall thin figure at the far end of the bar.

'You seem to know a hell of a lot for a man who got into town less than two days ago. You sure you ain't just a messenger boy for this Morgan soldier? Trying to scare the hell out of us?'

Then the thin man looked down at Alex McLagan, who was still being supported by his son. His coughing had stopped but he was still fighting to control his breathing.

'Do you trust this man, Alex?'

Matt found himself holding his breath as he turned to face the old man.

Which way would he go? He was surrounded by men who had paid him well to keep them out of reach of the law. One word from him and Matt Duggan would be gunned down where he stood.

Would a dying man keep his word? Or would he make one last gesture to show that the killers and robbers who had taken over the town that he was still one of them?

It was Max Benson who spoke out. 'Well, McLagan – what is it? Is this guy telling the truth?'

Struggling to his feet, the old man leaned heavily on Lance's shoulder. His voice was weak, barely above a whisper, but the silence that had fallen over the saloon as the men waited for his reply was total.

'This man rode in to town two days ago. Like the rest of you, he is running from the law. I have known him for four years or more and I have never had any reason to wonder why he came to Alvorado.' He paused and Matt was left wondering what was to come.

'He told me about the plans to send troops down from Fort Sedgwick and when that telegram arrived this morning it was proof that he was telling the truth. I believe him. And I have no reason to doubt that Morgan and his troops will be here by dawn. I would advise you not to be around when they arrive. You don't have to take my word but have I ever let you down? By this time tomorrow Alvorado will be a troop town.'

He slumped back into his chair and Matt felt the tension go out of his body. His speech over, McLagan turned to face Matt.

'That's all I can do for you, Brogan. Now I'm going to let my son take me home.'

Matt stepped aside and watched Lance help his father to his feet and out into the night. He followed them on to the sidewalk and looked on in silence as the young man struggled to lift the old man into his seat. He felt some sympathy for Lance – nobody could hold him responsible for the actions of his father or brother. There may have been evil in the family but it could not be laid at Lance's door.

Back inside the saloon, Max Benson was in deep discussion with the thin man who had challenged McLagan for the truth. Both men were trying to rally support for a stand of defiance against the troopers but there were no takers. Even the most hardened killers knew it would be suicide and one by one, then in pairs, they drifted outside. Battling against maybe a hundred or more heavily armed troopers was suicidal.

Matt's bluff was working. They were leaving town. He was about to head back to his hotel when he saw that a lamp was still shining in the sheriff's office across the street. He decided to stroll across and have a word with the sheriff. There was always the chance that he would learn something that would come in useful when the time for the showdown at the Big L arrived.

But there was another surprise in store when he pushed open the door and entered the office. The man sitting at the desk was Jed Harding.

CHAPTER FIFTEEN

Jed looked up from the sheet of paper he had been reading.

'Matt – come in, take a seat.'

Matt slid a chair across from the wall, placed it in front of the desk and sat down.

'Where's Leroy?'

'Gone I reckon,' Jed told him. 'The safe's empty, a couple of hundred dollars locked in the desk alongside a pile of wanted posters – most of them with the names of half the population of Alvorado on them I suspect. How did you get on with McLagan?'

'He's done his part,' said Matt, still puzzled why Harding was sitting at the sheriff's desk. 'He talked and they listened, and apart from one man – an ugly-looking brute by the name of Max Benson – they look to be heading out of town before the troopers arrive.'

Jed chuckled. 'Our ghost troopers from Fort Sedgwick. They believed that story. Good.'

'So that just leaves us the Big L crowd to deal with.'

'Guess so, but if I'm any judge the old man might just persuade some of the hotheads out there to back off and leave the farmers and homesteaders to get on with their lives.'

Jed nodded.

Matt got up from his chair and went over to pour himself a coffee from the stove.

'Alex knows he's dying and his young son Lance is a good kid. I don't think Alex wants to leave this earth without at least trying to make some things right.'

He paused before adding: 'If I'm right, that still leaves us with one problem even the all-powerful Alex McLagan can't solve.'

Jed knew what was coming. 'Would you pour me one of those?' he said, nodding towards the coffee pot. 'You're talking about his son, Roy, I guess.'

Matt slid the refilled mug on to the desk, spilling some of the coffee.

'You guess right, Jed.'

Harding made a half-hearted attempt to wipe away the spillage.

'We need to talk, Matt. Or should I say I need to talk and you need to listen.'

'Fine, I'm listening.'

There was nothing friendly in Matt's answer, though Jed hardly noticed. He had long suspected that Brogan had not taken their first meeting as a chance encounter on the trail to nowhere but so far he had not had the chance to challenge that suspicion. Now that time had arrived.

'There's something you've got to know, Matt.'

The other lowered his coffee cup. 'You said that like this was confession time.'

'In a way it is. Us being here is no accident. It was planned.'

'You've already explained all that and that you had a hand in it because I was sent down by a crooked judge. What else is there to tell me?'

Jed took a long drink of his coffee before answering.

Eventually, he said: 'Even though Henry Coburn was taking bribes, the Governor of the Penitentiary, well he. . . .'

'Jacob Harper!' Matt interrupted with a sneer.

'That's him. He would not cooperate with any plan. As far as he was concerned you were found guilty by a jury. He would have let you serve your fifteen years and come out a withered old man – if you survived that long. Nobody would have bothered about a man found guilty of murdering his family.

'While you were in the penitentiary that special law enforcement agency that President Grant put in force to fight corruption was given certain powers.

'So I took a chance on you, Matt. I had to get you out without the Governor knowing. He is not the sort of man to agree to anything that might go against his idea of Hell and Damnation coming down on the heads of men like you.

'I figured that if I could get you out and follow you, you would go in search of McLagan. We knew all about Alvorado and the department had heard rumours that the man who we believe killed my brother, a man we knew as Ray Shelby, could have been heading this way.

'It was a long shot but it looks as though it has paid off. When I came across you on the trail it gave me the chance to see the sort of man I was teaming up with – even though he didn't know I was.'

He paused to drink his coffee and to wait for Matt's reaction. He expected a display of anger – even violence. Instead, Matt Brogan remained calm. He even relaxed in his seat.

'I wondered when you would get round to telling me,' he said quietly.

Jed rested his elbows on the desk.

'You knew?'

'No, just guessed there was more to you than I was supposed to know. It was as though you were testing me out. You're a lawman so I waited for you to show your hand. And now you have.'

'Not quite all of it, my friend. I've got one more card to play. It's this.' He waved the paper he had been reading when Matt entered the office.

'I had to be sure of you and I am. So yesterday I had a friend send off a telegraph to my government department telling them what I had learned about you and making my recommendation. This is their answer. I collected it today.'

He handed the paper to Matt who read it without a word. When he had finished he passed it back to Jed.

'So, that's it,' he said. 'I'm a free man.'

'That's what clemency means, Matt. The appeal I made on your behalf has been granted. That friend I was telling you about. He works for the same agency I do. His name is Jim Bannon.'

Matt was silent. He was still digesting the news that he was no longer a hunted man – an escaped prisoner on the run. His thoughts were interrupted when Jed said: 'That leaves us with the question of what to do about Roy McLagan.'

Harding looked for an answer but was disappointed when Matt just shrugged.

'You're free now, Matt. If you want to stay out of jail you should leave young McLagan to me. He's wanted for murder, so you can let the law deal with him. And right now, around here I'm the only law they've got.'

'This isn't about the law, Jed. It's between me and the McLagan clan. The old man's dying and young Lance is no killer. That leaves Roy and the Mexican. They killed my family.'

Harding got up from his seat and leaned forward, his face stopping only inches in front of Matt.

'Don't be a fool!' he snapped. 'Are they worth going back to jail for? To find yourself on the end of a noose?' His voice rose with every word. 'Is that what you want?'

Matt didn't answer. He was thinking about a blind man named Sam Dawson and his daughter Jemma, and her husband who was making her life a misery. He had promised to return the gun and the horse plus what was left of the cash he had taken.

The thought prompted him to say: 'You are not going after McLagan alone. You need me and the others. Is that right?'

'You know I do, so?'

'Deputize me. Deputize all of us. Make us the law.'

Jed Harding sank into his chair and thought about the suggestion. Before he could speak, Matt added: 'It would make us a posse, all legal.'

Jed looked his new friend straight in the eye. 'What you're asking is for me to give you a badge to kill Roy McLagan.'

Matt held up his hand. 'No, Jed, what I'm saying is that if you want my help it doesn't come free of charge. You said yourself I can ride out of here a free man with a paper to prove it and that would leave you with what – a group of angry farmers who don't know what they are letting themselves in for. It's your choice and what have you got to lose?'

Before Harding could reply there was the sound of a gunshot out in the street. Then another. And then a whole burst of gunfire.

Both men hurried across to the window. Outside a crowd of gun-waving men on horseback were firing at anything that took their eye, smashing street lights and store windows, yelling and firing into the night while others, all filled with rotgut whisky, looted the stores. Leading the crowd of troublemakers was Max Benson.

'It's their way of saying farewell to Alvorado,' Jed said, moving back towards his desk. After several minutes the yelling and the shooting stopped and Matt stood and watched as they all rode out of town and into the night. Even Benson was on his way.

But the peace on Alvorado's streets was only brief. Matt and Jed were still discussing their plans for the visit to the Big L when the door burst open and a frantic Jonathon Elwell staggered into the office.

Breathless and with a look of terror in his eyes, he gasped: 'It's happening again. They're burning down Bill Coley's place!'

CHAPTER SIXTEEN

By the time Jed and Matt reached the Coley farm the house was nothing more than a smouldering ruin.

Bill Coley stood with his wife and son, Joey, his life wrecked by the raiders' attack. He could not hide the hate in his voice as he explained what happened.

'There were six of them – all masked – and they dragged my wife and Joey out of their beds and forced us to watch as they torched my home piece by piece.'

'You didn't recognize any of them?' Jed asked after a lengthy time Coley spent consoling his wife and son.

'They were all masked but they were Big L men that's for sure,' the distraught man said at last. 'They may have hidden their faces but they couldn't hide that Big L brand on their horses. And I'm sure one of them was that mean sonofabitch Roy McLagan.'

'There were six of them?' Matt asked, looking for confirmation.

Coley nodded. 'No more than that.'

'If it's the same men who burned Caleb's place to the ground that will be the strength of young McLagan's group. The rest of the ranch hands must be just that – cowboys,' Matt said.

Jed agreed. 'That evens things up.'

The two men exchanged glances. 'Tomorrow we ride out to the Big L.'

The small group rode in silence. They left the town before dawn and the sun was still low in the eastern sky when they arrived at the boundary fence of the McLagan ranch.

Matt Brogan had been grateful for the thinking time that the hour-long ride had offered. In the days since his escape from the penitentiary – an escape he now knew had been organized by the man leading the short column of riders across the New Mexico flatlands – his emotions had changed.

He had fled from the roadwork gang with hate in his heart for the men who had killed his family. Hate and anger. But now . . . for the old man there was even a sense of pity.

But there was still enough hate left for McLagan's son and the Mexican Herrera, and although he had listened to Jed Harding's reasons for taking Roy McLagan alive and had promised not to interfere, he was not sure he would keep that promise.

Harding, at the head of the column, suddenly raised his hand and called a halt to the procession. Turning in the saddle, he spoke to the group.

'Remember, men. We are here to talk. There will be no guns unless they want to get in our way. We have got to be ready for that. I want Roy McLagan taken alive. He's wanted for murder and robbery and I'm here to see that the law is carried out.'

'The law weren't much use to me,' Caleb retaliated. 'It didn't stop them burning my place down and killing my stock. I ain't disposed to be talkative about that, Mr Harding.'

'Listen, all of you. We are not a lynch mob. You've all

been deputized and anybody who doesn't like the rules can ride out of here now. You may be needed back in town if things don't go according to plan here.'

Nobody moved.

Jed took the silence as agreement and, without another word, turned back in his saddle and nudged his horse into motion. The others followed. But their arrival at the Big L had not gone unnoticed. High on a ridge, two riders watched the short procession heading through the gates less than a mile from the big house.

Mitch Buller leaned forward and scratched his head.

'What d'ya reckon, Mex? Do you think we ought to go down? Looks like the boss may need a couple of extra guns?'

Herrera grinned, rubbed his stubble and tried to swat away a few annoying bugs.

'Mitch, my friend, we go on down to the house and we tell Roy what we have seen and we say we have come to help. And then we find ourselves trying to explain to him about how you killed the sheriff and took all the money. What do you think our friend will say to that?'

Buller looked as though he had been hit by a raging bull.

'Hell, Mex. Roy don't have to know about Quince and the money.'

The Mexican snorted. 'And you don't think he will find out that we have taken $5,000 each from the dead sheriff?

'So, what is it you are saying, Mex?'

'What I am saying Mitch is that a man can be many miles away from the Big L and Alvorado with $5,000 in his belt.'

Without another word, Herrera drew his pistol and fired twice into the chest of the unsuspecting Buller.

As the dead man hit the ground, the Mexican dismounted and knelt down to retrieve Mitch's share of the money. Stuffing the bills into his shirt, he got back to his feet and stood by his horse to watch the riders far below as they headed towards the big farmhouse.

Then he remounted, turned his horse and headed down the slope and in the opposite direction, without so much as a backward glance or an *adios*.

By this time tomorrow he would be home in Mexico.

A lone figure stood on the verandah of the house as the six riders pulled up at the hitching rail. He was pointing a rifle at his visitors.

'That's far enough, you men.'

Alex McLagan was leaning against a post but that was the only sign that he was not the man who had built a cattle empire and run a private town as a hole in the wall hide-away for outlaws.

'Turn your horses around and get off my ranch – there's nothing for you here, Brogan.'

'We've no more argument with you, Alex. It's Roy we want – and his Mexican friend.'

McLagan moved away from the post but it was an effort to stand upright and straight-backed.

'Now, listen you farmers, I don't know what this lawman and Brogan have been telling you but I've asked you to leave. Now I am telling you. Last night I did Brogan's bidding and I gave you back your town. But if you think I'm going to give you my son so you can hang him then you're a bunch of fools. I'll shoot the first man who makes a move towards the house.'

Only Jed Harding made any move and that was just to lean forward in his saddle.

'There'll be no lynching, Alex. Roy will get a fair trial. You have my word on that.'

'Your word maybe, but what about the rest of them? You

sure they aren't itching for my boy's neck?'

'Your son burned my house down and killed my stock.' Caleb shouted back.

Alex McLagan lowered his rifle as though it had become a heavy weight in his hands.

'If you've got proof of that then bring the sheriff. Let him sort it out. If you can prove it, I'll pay for your dead cattle. And your house. But you're not getting my son. Not unless you're ready to kill me first.'

'Well, there's the thing, Alex. We can't find your tame sheriff anywhere. He's left town and with a lot of cash like it's for good.'

Before the old man could answer, he was joined on the verandah by his younger son.

It was Lance who spoke. 'You are wasting your time here. Roy's not in the house. He hasn't been home for two days. We don't know where he is.'

Family loyalty was not totally dead and buried in the McLagan house.

'We'll find him, Alex. Sooner or later, Roy's going to answer for his crimes. It would be better for him if the law found him before anybody else. There are people out there who won't be in any hurry to give him a fair trial.'

Jed turned his horse and signaled for the others to follow. But nobody moved. Instead with anger reaching boiling point, it was Caleb who yelled: 'Your boy's going to pay, McLagan! You tell him if he steps into town he better be ready to use that fancy gun of his.'

'I ordered you off my land, Brogan. That was your last warning. Get your hides out of here or I'll get my men to run you off.'

He fired his rifle into the air. Suddenly it was followed by a hail of gunfire. It came from the direction of the barn. Behind Jed one of the horses reared up and the rider fell to the ground, clutching his shoulder. In an instant there was havoc. The riders leapt from their saddles and raced for cover behind an abandoned wagon.

Matt, instead of following the rest, ran up the steps, brushing aside the two men on the verandah and snatched the rifle from the old man's feeble grasp before diving into the house.

Spinning round to face the startled trio, he snarled: 'You set this ambush, Alex. You're no better than Roy.'

'No!' the old man protested. 'I swear I didn't know. I swear to God I thought Roy was out on the range.'

Matt had to think fast. Outside there was a rapid exchange of gunfire and he knew that Jed and the others would be massacred if it went on much longer.

'Then prove it. Get out there and call them off. Move!'

'Pa, don't listen to him. You'll be killed if you go out there. Your life won't be worth two cents.'

Alex put his arm around Lance's shoulder in rare show of fatherly affection.

'How much is it worth now, son? I'm sick and I haven't got too long left to put something right. Three years ago we took this man's family and home away from him. He came here to kill me and Roy and the Mexican. Instead, he helped you to save my life. Well, now he can have me and the Mexican but Roy, he is your brother – I will not see him gunned down, no matter what he has done. Like you he is my son.'

Lance made another move to protest but his father waved him aside. Unsteadily, he made his way outside. The exchange of gunfire was still raging as he stepped out into the morning sunlight.

Out front, Jed and a small group of the farmers he knew only by sight – the McLagans had never bothered to learn the names of their neighbours – were crouched behind the frame of an old wagon. Another was slumped beside the corral fence clutching his shoulder. Alex's fading eyesight meant that he was unable to see the extent of the man's injury but he was hardly moving.

Thirty yards away across the dusty square several figures were half hidden behind the framework of the barn. There was no sign of Roy.

Alex leaned on the post and tried desperately to gather his strength. Eventually he found his voice to shout: 'You men in the barn hold your fire. Harding, tell your men to do the same.'

Jed raised his arm to signal to the others to lower their weapons. He did not know what the old man had in mind but he had to be given the chance to stop a massacre.

But before McLagan could speak again there was a shout from inside the barn.

'Stay out of this, Alex! We've already been given our orders.'

McLagan stiffened. 'Who's that? I gave no orders.'

'It's Clay Wells, Alex. And Roy's told us what we have to do if those farmers came trespassing on the Big L. We're going to run them off.'

Matt, still crouching under cover inside the house, looked up at Lance.

'Who is Clay Wells?'

'He's one of Roy's drinking buddies.'

Alex McLagan was trying to keep calm between the two rival groups.

'Listen to me all of you! Roy isn't the boss here yet. Not while I'm still alive. I'm ordering you to put down your guns.'

Jed Harding signaled to his men to keep calm. He sensed something was about to happen. And he did not have long to wait.

Suddenly, a shower of bullets rained down from the loft of the barn. It did not take years of experience as a lawman in tight situations to know that this could become a bloodbath.

He looked round. A quick glance was more than enough to convince him that the small group who had enthusiastically joined his hurriedly assembled posse of deputies were no longer convinced that there was anything to be gained at the Big L.

Somehow Jed had to get them out of there. Crouching behind the abandoned wagon, he crept towards the fencing that surrounded the corral. Out of sight of the men in the barn, he signaled to the nearest man to back slowly away.

But the lull in the shooting was all too brief. A spray of bullets peppered the fencing of the corral and splintered the wheels of the wagon.

Then there was silence again.

Across the yard, Alex had made his way down the steps with Lance's help and faced the barn. When he spoke, his voice was surprisingly strong.

'Roy! You in there? Come on out, son, we've got to talk.'

No answer.

'Either you come out or I'm coming in.' More silence. 'What's it gonna be, son?'

All eyes were on the old man as he started to walk slowly towards the barn. But he had only gone a few steps when Roy McLagan appeared at the opening in the barn's hayloft.

'That's far enough, Pa.'

The old man stopped and stood in silence. Who would make the next move? Matt Brogan, crouching behind the railing on the verandah, could feel the tension in the air. The old man was unarmed, Roy was pointing a rifle at his father's chest. There was a sneer in the son's voice when he eventually spoke.

'You're through giving orders around here. You're too old. You've forgotten what made us who we are. This is McLagan land. You told me that. You taught me – but not anymore. From now on, I'm the one giving the orders and that includes getting rid of these sod-busting homesteaders.'

'Listen Roy. Son.' There was pleading in the old man's voice. 'These people – they were here before we arrived. We can't just take what is theirs.'

Roy McLagan spat.

'When did you ever worry about that? You took what you wanted and you told me to do the same. Well that's what I'm doing.'

Alex McLagan's shoulders sagged.

'Times have changed, Roy. What was right then, ain't right now. It's wrong. I was wrong about lots of things.'

Roy McLagan remained unmoved. And his anger was rising.

'Remember what you told me. Nobody owes us anything. Take what we want because nobody gives us a thing. Do you remember that, old man?'

'I remember it, Roy, I do but, listen to me, tell your men to put up their guns so we can talk.'

Roy tightened his grip on the rifle. 'We've got nothing to say anymore. You've gone soft in your old age and— '

Suddenly Alex found fresh strength in his voice and yelled back: 'I'm dying, son. God help me, can't you see I'm dying?'

For a moment it seemed as though he had managed to get through to his son but any hope of that disappeared almost immediately, with his son's next words.

'We all have to die some day, which is why I am giving

the orders now. The best thing you can do is take that so-called brother of mine and get out. Find yourself some shack far away from here. You're no kin of mine any more. And tell that kid he can have the girl – I ain't got any use for her.'

With that, he raised his rifle and fired at the feet of Lance, the bullet sending a spray of dust over his boots. Then he turned and went back into the barn.

Lance gripped his father's arm and led him back to the house. Matt greeted him as the pair reached the top of the steps.

'I'm sorry, Brogan. You saw I tried. You saw it all. Roy's in charge now. You helped to save my life for nothing.' He went into the house but as he crossed the threshold he turned.

'Listen, I'd like to say that Roy is no son of mine but that would be wrong. He is exactly that – he's a McLagan.'

CHAPTER SEVENTEEN

Matt Brogan watched the old man sink into an armchair, exhausted, broken and beaten. Lance stood by, a look of desolation on his young face.

Matt felt the anger rising. It was time to put Lance to the test. Was he just another version of his older brother? Did he really care what was happening to the McLagan name or his home?

He gripped the younger man's arms and shook him violently.

'Listen, son and listen good.' He glanced down at the old man. 'Your father has not got long. He knows it, I know it – hell, boy, even you know it.'

Lance stood over his father and Matt could see that he was close to breaking down.

'What can I do? Tell me, Brogan. Help me.'

Matt slackened his grip.

'You may as well know, not everybody is going to walk out of here, son. There will be killings. I don't think Roy is going to throw down his guns, do you?'

Ten minutes passed before another burst of gunfire outside came as a reminder that there would be more shooting to come.

Lance shook his head in despair.

Matt pressed on: 'That means you have got to decide whose side you are on in this.'

'He's my brother,' Lance said but it was a feeble attempt at protest.

'You heard what he said out there. He doesn't care for you or the girl, or even your father.' He paused again, waiting for his words to sink in. 'He's no good, Lance. I know that better than anybody. He's the reason I came here.

'You can't pretend you don't know what they did – your brother, father and that Mexican Herrera.'

Lance remembered the newspaper cutting he had taken from the drawer in the sheriff's office. He studied his father and then, as if coming to a decision, he turned to face Brogan.

'What is it you want me to do to help?'

'Nothing! You'll do nothing, little boy! Like you always do.'

The voice was harsh, sneering. But the answer had not come from Matt Brogan. Standing in the open doorway at the rear of the house, rifle in hand, was Roy.

'Surprised to see me, are you, Brogan? You should have known you couldn't rely on a bunch of old women. All I had to do was come round the back of the barn and . . . here I am.'

'And you're going to kill us all? Is that your next move?'

'Not all. Just you. The old man here is dying without any help from me and what happens to Lance doesn't matter to me. He's not fit to be called a McLagan. It's what we should have done three years ago but the old man was already going soft in the head. He was the one who went through that phony trial when we should have just thrown you in the fire with the woman and the kid.'

Matt stiffened, his jaw muscles tightening and his fist clenching as he stared into the eyes of the man with the gun. Keep him talking . . . let him gloat and sneer, think he was enjoying his moment, it was Matt's only chance of leaving the ranch alive.

'It would have saved us a whole heap of trouble, though I must give the old man some credit. Seeing you squirm when the judge gave that excuse for a jury his summing up which told them what they had to decide, well . . . I enjoyed that.'

'You can kill me, sure enough,' Matt said quietly. 'But I'm not the only one to track you down, am I? And you are fast running out of friends, Roy. Your tame sheriff has gone; even your trusty Mexican has cleared out. You'll soon be all alone.'

'Like you are now, eh, Brogan? Well, at least I'm still alive to buy myself a few more Mexicans. And they come cheap out here. If you've got anything else to say then keep it for your Maker.'

He raised the rifle. . . .

The gunshot shattered the silence; the bullet ripped into his stomach and he let out a scream as he crashed to the floor, his eyes wide open in horror as the blood rushed through his fingers.

For a moment, nobody spoke as the three men watched him die.

'I couldn't let him do it, Pa. I couldn't just stand by and let Roy destroy us all.'

Lance slumped into the nearest chair and let the gun that had just killed his brother slide from his fingers.

CHAPTER EIGHTEEN

There were two funerals that day and the small graveyard was crowded with townsfolk. But there were few mourners among them as the bodies of Alex McLagan and his son Roy were laid side by side while the Reverend Elwell said a few words over the coffins. Instead, the crowds had gathered only to witness the end of a dynasty that had ruled their lives for too long. Nearby were two other McLagan graves, Alice and Nell, the two wives of the patriarch of the Big L.

Alex had grown old and rich on the strength of hired guns and gamblers as well as fugitives who had turned Alvorado into a town of shame where murder and mayhem were part of everyday life. A town ruled by fear. There were few tears shed in the cemetery that morning. But the celebration was muted – the people of Alvorado were still uncertain of what the future held.

Lance and Amy Bannon stood close by while Jed Harding and Matt Brogan kept their distance.

The shootout at the Big L had ended when Alex McLagan managed to recover enough strength to step outside and tell the cowhands still inside the barn that Roy was dead – that their fight with the homesteaders was over.

That same night, after a day of mourning over his dead

son, Alex McLagan died in his sleep.

Now, two days later, the groups drifted away from the cemetery and residents of the small town of Alvorado no longer needed to live in fear.

Jed Harding and Matt Brogan walked side by side down the hill towards the town, closely followed by the reverend.

There was no sign of the phantom soldiers . . . and Max Benson and the rest had deserted their hideaway. The bluff had worked – Alex McLagan had ended his life doing one good thing.

'What plans do you have now?' the clergyman put in as he stepped up his pace to join them. 'I take it you will both be heading out of Alvorado.'

Jed and Matt exchanged glances.

For one, there was the task of restoring law and order to this remote New Mexico town.

Harding turned to face the clergyman.

'This town needs a new lawman, Reverend. I thought I knew just the man to pin on a star but it seems I was mistaken.' He looked at Matt. 'He has other plans.'

Matt Brogan did not answer. He and Jed had spent the previous night talking about the future. There was nothing more to be said.

The following morning, Matt rode out of town without looking back. He was a free man but he still had some unfinished business to settle. Somehow he would find his way back to the remote farm and fulfil the promise he made to Sam Dawson that he would return the clothes and the cash he had taken from the bedroom cupboard.

For the first time in more than three years Matt Brogan felt there was something left in his life.